Stories

For my long-suffering wife,
who manages my constant daydreams and delusions
with enviable grace

For Nono,
whose stories inspired me to write my own

For all of you
who give of your precious time
to read my work

Big head, target for enemy. Big heart, target for friend.

—Confucious

Preface

Writing is as close as we get to keeping a hold on the thousand and one things—childhood, certainties, cities, doubts, dreams, instants, phrases, parents, loves—that go on slipping, like sand, through our fingers.

—Salman Rushdie, *Imaginary Homelands*

My first public embarrassment happened as a 10-year-old being asked to translate what the old man waving his arms and screaming at me in Spanish from the sideline of my youth soccer game was saying. Nono, my maternal grandfather, has never been one to keep his mouth shut or refer to people by their birth names. So for as long as I can remember, he's called me *Cabezón*—literally, Big Head.

At that age, I had no way of knowing that in Argentina nicknames like *Cabezón* or *Piojo* (Louse), my brother's, and *Enano* (Dwarf), my dad's, are common and inoffensive—because we weren't in Argentina. My parents and grandparents had left in the 1980s to settle in Bayonne, New Jersey, a working-class city a stone's throw from Manhattan, where I was born and they have lived ever since. At every soccer game, Nono paced the sideline, shadowing my movements on the field. His agitation was obvious: for miles anyone with functioning ears could hear him shouting for me to play the offside trap or dribble the ball upfield, and lamenting when I failed to properly execute his strategy for cutting down an opponent without the referee pulling out a yellow card. Each instruction or critique he punctuated with a thunderous *Cabezón*, as if my ears were stuffed with cotton balls and I was the only person in the world who couldn't hear him.

When you wake up every morning balancing an Easter Island statue on your neck, your skin must be as thick as your neck muscles are strong. Mine is barely thicker than cellophane. It's taken two decades for me to come to terms with my most prominent physical feature. Because it wasn't just Nono who noticed. Talk of my head size crossed language barriers. In high school, Mickey, one of my best friends, conspired with Dan Kidd to debut two new nicknames for me: Tipsy and Jenga. (I guess I wasn't doing as good a job at the balancing act as I thought.) Any time they'd shout them in the hallways, I'd immediately tense up. I was a teenager with raging hormones doing everything I could to attract a girlfriend. And there they were, stacking the odds against me by placing a magnifying glass on my biggest insecurity.

My junior year, I tried a diversionary tactic. I grew my hair out past my chin and wore it swept over one side of my face like emo kids did in the suburbs. When that didn't work, I dyed it black. That failed too. So I tried imitating a young Antonio Banderas, wearing my hair back and over my ears to my shoulders or tied in a slick ponytail. But nothing worked. Fed up one afternoon, I announced on Myspace that one day the people of Bayonne would regret calling me Tipsy. Soon after, though, I conceded the fight. I accepted that in New Jersey and Argentina, some people will always choose to show their love through a fist aimed directly at your heart. The sting from the punch is how you can be sure it's beating. I also accepted that having a supersized head doesn't mean I was gifted with exceptional intellect. Instead of smarts, God gave me longings, big and small, that I've hoarded for decades. Stacked on top of one another, they reach as high as the Eiffel Tower.

As a boy, I wanted to be both a New York Yankee and the next Gabriel Batistuta. I watched nature shows by the Kratt Brothers on PBS and imagined working in foreign countries as a marine biologist or tracking cheetahs on the African plain. I traveled the world, even if it was only in my mind. Sometimes I was the bassist in a punk band, other times a writer in a European bar drinking whiskey and wearing a tweed sports coat with patches on the elbows. I was always in search of the road less traveled. Now, in my mid-30s, I'm still searching, wondering whether I'll be brave enough to take that road when it finally appears. I write these stories because I refuse to believe I'm alone in this struggle.

Nothing is extraordinary about my life or achievements so far—certainly not enough to warrant publishing a book. But the simple fact is that there's nothing else I can do well enough to keep the candle wick burning at night. I recently lamented to my father-in-law, "Why did God pick this thorn to stick in my side? Wouldn't I be happier selling used cars or life insurance?" *Why must I write?*

I started writing as a boy, around the same age I was when my grandfather yelled at me from the sidelines of a soccer field at Hudson County Park. Through bad poems scribbled on lined notebook paper, teenage song lyrics about female rejection, and blogs where I ranted about American politics and modern soccer tactics, I longed to be read. I can't explain why.

Beside each other in bed this past spring, my wife, Haley, and I got to talking about the future. She presented me with a straightforward scenario: "You could own a house and retire with a million dollars in the bank but never publish anything, or you can die broke and write a book." I chose the latter. "You realize that's not what a *normal person* would choose, right?" she responded with all the love she—a normal person—could muster.

I often wish I were the kind of person capable of shutting up and being happy with a steady paycheck and a hobby or two. But no matter how many jobs I work or how many times I visit a new soccer stadium or walk a sandy bank with a fishing pole in hand, I still stumble through my front door eager to sit down at my laptop with a cup of coffee, turn on a Spotify playlist, and pour my thoughts out in a Google Doc.

I'm sure most people don't wake up with the urge to tell strangers that they don't know how to change a flat tire or use power tools, or that they once pooped themselves while sick with a stomach bug, or that every time their wife leaves them alone in the house they spiral into thinking about the dozens of ways they might die before 40. But for some reason, I do. Which begs the question: *Are people with average-sized heads afflicted in the same way that I am?*

Maybe the chaos that brews each waking minute within its borders is the reason why I was assigned a head of such great size: God needed the space to work. And despite what I thought all those years ago, I'm still growing into the thing.

Knoxville, Tennessee
August 2023

The Penalty Kick

Hold fast to dreams
For if dreams die
Life is a broken-winged bird
That cannot fly.

—Langston Hughes

Just as I do today, I spent a lot of my time as a boy wandering through daydreams. For anyone who grows up in a family of sports lovers, it's common for one of these dreams to be of some heroic moment achieved on the world's biggest stage. Mine was scoring a World Cup–winning penalty kick. I wrote the script for it while lying with my eyes closed in bed or walking to 16th Street Park with a ball tucked under my arm.

Like the other 8 billion people on the planet, I could not have foreseen when I wrote a fictionalized version of my heroic moment and published it online on May 2, 2018, that four years later the final of the men's World Cup in Qatar would come down to a penalty kick.

As a lifelong Argentina supporter, I hoped dearly that it wouldn't. But God has a sense of humor. As this was my first big-headed delusion, I think it makes for an appropriate opener to this collection of stories.

Jacob Costa gathered the ball from the back of the net and carried it 12 paces toward a spot he had picked out in the dirt in front of the goal.

He dug his toe in and stamped the ground hard. Jacob didn't want the ball to budge once he had set it. Satisfied, he leaned over and placed the ball gently into the dirt pocket. He examined it for a second, then lifted it about a foot from the ground and spun it carefully in his hands before placing it back onto the dirt. Jacob's dad had taught him to always set the ball down this way. "Never let the referee do it for you," he had told him one afternoon as they practiced before a big game. "It's your penalty kick—not theirs."

Every day for three weeks, Jacob had watched World Cup games on TV with his grandfather. At the final whistle, he would sprint to the basement, grab a black-and-white soccer ball, then march down to the small park behind his parents' house to kick the ball until the floodlights came on. The lights signaled to Jacob that soon the adults would show up and that he had to go home. After rushing through dinner, Jacob spent the hour before sunset on the porch with the ball in his hands, watching curiously as older men hopped the yellow brick wall at the end of his street on their way to play soccer with their friends. They were mostly laborers from Mexico and Central America, and they wore jerseys Jacob recognized from the TV broadcasts: the dark green of Mexico, luminescent yellow of Brazil, and deep red of Spain.

The sun on his back in the stifling mid-July heat, Jacob took a step away from the ball and lifted his eyes toward the goal. The once-white net was now a dusty gray and hanging sadly, full of holes. After taking a deep breath, he lifted his gaze to the sky and made the sign of the cross.

"It all comes down to this," he heard the voice of the British commentator Ian Darke say. *"Jacob Costa is going to be the last man to the spot for Argentina."* (In his head, he always played for Argentina. It was the team his dad and grandfather cheered for when they watched together in the kitchen.)

Standing behind the ball, Jacob lowered his gaze. He calculated: three steps back and another to the left. With each movement, he felt as if he was stepping backward in time, transported to the Maracanã Stadium in Rio de Janeiro on the eve of the 1950 World Cup final between Brazil and Uruguay. Jacob turned his back and stared into the distance, imagining 200,000 people in the stands. That day, Uruguay miraculously came from behind to beat the hosts 2–1 in their backyard. His grandfather had told him the story many times. Supposedly, the Brazilian fans threw themselves to their deaths after losing the final. Across the country, the news reported heart attacks and suicides after the final whistle.

Jacob inhaled through his nose, exhaled hard, and turned to face the goal again.

"Costa has been Argentina's most consistent penalty taker. He hasn't missed from the spot all year. But can he do it on the big stage here? Millions around the world are watching, asking themselves the same question: Will Jacob Costa be the hero for Argentina?"

Jacob scowled; his eyes narrowed. He was meters from the most fearsome goalkeeper he could imagine. A Frankenstein-esque creation—a mix of Gianluigi Buffon, Edwin van der Sar, and Hugo Lloris—returned the glare. Jacob ran his left hand through his hair, which was drenched in sweat, and stared into the imaginary stands brimming with hordes of fans tensely awaiting his next move.

Filling his lungs with air, Jacob focused his gaze on the goalkeeper in his mind. He was bouncing around, taunting him, like a boxer dancing in the corner before throwing the first punch. Jacob smirked. He strode toward the ball, planted his left foot beside it, then drove a powerful shot that curved just inside the top right corner of the goal and through a hole in the net. Immediately, Jacob collapsed to his knees in the dirt. He raised his fists to heaven and buried his head in his hands, crying real tears.

"He's done it! Jacob Costa has done it! He's won the World Cup for Argentina with the very last kick of the match!"

The floodlights came on as Jacob kneeled in the dirt, imagining his teammates surrounding him. He felt their phantom embrace and heard the reverberations from the delirious throbbing of the people shouting in the stands. The ball was 20 yards away in a ditch beside the trees. It was time to go home.

Becoming Batistuta

I n Mrs. Squittieri's history class during my eighth-grade year at PS 14, we read excerpts from Greek mythology and one day, in the way of great teachers past and present, she prompted us with the question "What does it mean to be a hero?" In the ensuing discussion, Mrs. Squittieri stepped to the board at the front of the room and charted a course in chalk from Odysseus, Hercules, and Achilles to the heroes we as 13-year-olds looked up to. Then she told us to write a report about one of our choosing.

I wrote mine about Gabriel Batistuta—an Argentinian soccer player who, in the 1990s and early 2000s, would have passed for Italian Jesus (or *Jesus* Jesus, if you grew up Catholic) and was for many years the greatest goalscorer in the world.

From birth, the first people we look up to are our parents. They feed and clothe us when we can't do it for ourselves—and, if you grew up in an immigrant family, as I did, for many years afterward. They put a roof over our heads, drive us to rehearsals and sports practices, and pay the water bill without griping about how long our showers take. But there comes a point in all of our lives, once we understand better who we are and what space we want to create for ourselves in the world, that something changes. This transition comes before teenage rebellion, before realizing that our parents may have their own rich inner lives and—much later—that they may know more than we give them credit for. My parents watched it happen with me as I'll watch it happen with my children when their needs extend beyond the immediate. Soon they'll pick new heroes who can meet the acute longings they feel but may not yet have the words to articulate.

Batistuta has long held a special place in my heart. I proudly enlarged his picture for the cover of my eighth-grade report. I chose the same picture for my first Facebook cover image in December 2014. In it, he's wearing the sky blue and white of Argentina, balling his fists in the air, his golden mane whipping in the wind as he celebrates one of 56 goals he'd put into the back of the net during his 11-year national team career.

I first learned of Batistuta during the 1994 World Cup. Nono, my maternal grandfather, who lives with my grandmother in the apartment downstairs from my parents, was at work during most of the group stage games, so she taped them for him to watch while they ate dinner. I was five years old then. All I knew about sports was soccer and the Argentinian national team.

I loved watching Batistuta, who loomed over his defenders, his hair like a superhero's cape behind him. He hit the ball so hard that the TV seemed to be stuck in fast-forward for seconds after it left his boot. At the 1994 tournament in the US, Batigol (as fans called him) scored a hat trick in the opening game against Greece, then once more from the penalty spot as Argentina was eliminated by Romania in the Round of 16. At the 1998 World Cup in France, Batistuta scored the winning goal in the opening match against Japan, then added a hat trick in Argentina's 5–0 decimation of Jamaica. In that game, his third goal, a penalty kick, was the most powerfully hit shot I've ever seen. He scored in the second-round win over England, a game best remembered for David Beckham seeing red after kicking out at Diego Simeone. Then came the quarterfinal against the Netherlands.

I was three feet from the wooden TV console at our vacation home in the Pocono Mountains as Argentina was eliminated 2–1. I remember it like yesterday. Dennis Bergkamp scored in the 90th minute, moments after Ariel Ortega was sent off for headbutting Edwin van der Sar. My dad had invited his Portuguese friends to eat barbecue and watch the game with us. It was July 4, the day we celebrate American independence with fireworks. I held my head in my hands, trying to hold back tears as mucus dripped from my nose.

It was much harder to watch international club soccer games in the age before streaming services became ubiquitous. So I spent much of the year in a deficit of soccer consumption. Highlights from games played in the US weren't even shown on ESPN—and Batistuta played his club soccer an ocean away, in Italy, for Fiorentina and Roma. But it didn't matter to me what club he played for or when, as long as he lined up for the national anthem when Argentina beckoned.

For most of his career, Batistuta wore the No. 9 jersey, traditionally assigned to center forwards: hulking, aggressive goalscorers who rarely cross midfield to defend. Even though I was a slow, stocky center-back, I asked for the same jersey number on all my teams, and my American coaches usually gave it to me without a fuss. By the time Mrs. Squittieri assigned us to write about our heroes, I had stopped playing in organized youth leagues and was instead going to 16th Street Park to play pickup soccer every night with the Latin American laborers who came out once the floodlights came on. I was shyer than I am now. But when an Ecuadorian named Armando, the unofficial organizer of our Sunday games, asked my name, I said, "You can call me Batistuta."

The nickname stuck until I left Bayonne in 2011, my GPS set to Knoxville, Tennessee, where I've lived ever since. I packed a pair of cleats for the first couple of drives home for Thanksgiving and Christmas. But it wasn't the same once I got to the field. Some of the old faces had also gone, and I realized you can't go back in time, no matter how badly you may want to. A few years ago, a Mexican friend I hadn't seen since college met my mom at an Italian bakery in town and remembered fondly the nights we spent together at the park—except he couldn't recall my real name. To him and the other regulars, I was and will always be Batistuta.

My hero played his last international soccer game at the 2002 World Cup in Japan. It was the third of the group stage against Sweden. The game was broadcast at 2:30 in the morning on a school night; I set an alarm so I wouldn't miss it. In agony, I watched from the spare bedroom as Nono watched from the kitchen. Only his occasional bursts of outrage at the players and referees broke the silence. After losing to England the game before, Argentina—a favorite to win the tournament after cruising through South American qualifiers with a single loss—had to beat the Swedes to advance. Instead, they tied 1–1 and were eliminated. When I close my eyes to remember that morning, I see a much younger me lying prone on the bed, moaning for someone to rescue him from the pain, like my toddler when he rouses in the middle of the night screaming for milk.

How in the world was I expected to fall back to sleep if my hero was no longer in the World Cup? If I had a choice in the matter, I would've stayed in bed and moped until 2006. My mom and grandmother would've tended to me as though I'd been struck down by some mysterious illness that left me capable of consuming only mashed potatoes and Sprite through a straw for the next 48 hours. But instead I was forced to go to school in the aftermath of the Great Elimination, just as my dad and Nono had to get up and go to work despite the anguish.

Even though I walked into homeroom looking like a zombie, no one asked what was wrong. I built a fortress of protection with my arms and lowered my head, still throbbing with grief and exhaustion, to the desk, where it stayed for the remainder of seventh grade. Fortunately for me, American kids didn't care much for professional soccer before Landon Donovan's last-minute goal against Algeria at the 2010 World Cup in South Africa. By then the English Premier League had made its way onto American cable, and every budding soccer fan knew Kun Agüero, Carlos Tevez, and Fabricio Coloccini.

The morning of Argentina's humiliation, before modern technology brought soccer to everyone, no one at my school knew of Batistuta. I was stranded on a desert island with my obsession. And I'm grateful for it. Because if France had beaten Argentina in the World Cup final in 2022, I'm sure my phone would have lit up with Twitter notifications and phone calls from loved ones worried about my health. I would've tossed it into the Tennessee River—and even that wouldn't have kept me from waking up drenched in sweat after imagining Kylian Mbappé beating me with a stale baguette from atop the Eiffel Tower, his French henchmen surrounding my broken body and snickering like hyenas. The endless memes and GIFs of Lionel Messi in tears, just as Batistuta had been in Japan, would've destroyed me.

I wrote my report for Mrs. Squittieri one year before my hero retired from professional soccer. After the World Cup, he moved to Qatar for one final season, breaking the record for most goals scored in a league campaign: 25 in 18 games. That was 20 years ago. I was still a kid. Since then, I've finished high school and college, married, moved away, divorced, gone to grad school, changed careers, remarried, and became a father thrice over. I've watched a million hours of soccer on screens and in stadiums. On car rides to the pet cemetery with Nono, who wouldn't let me listen to the radio, I learned about *El Conejo* Saviola and Juan Román Riquelme, who came after Batistuta and were supposed to be a part of the generation that would finally return the national team to glory. I bought imitation jerseys with my last name on the back from a Colombian at the Meadowlands Flea Market, spent $1,500 on a flight home to watch Argentina lose a goalless Copa América Final in penalty kicks to Chile in 2016, and spoke face-to-face with Mario Kempes—the player who led Argentina to its first World Cup victory in 1978—under fluorescent lighting at ESPN headquarters in Bristol, Connecticut.

I've watched Argentina crash out of World Cups from TV sets in Bayonne, Bristol, and at a Bolivian friend's house in Knoxville. That last time, I wasn't as heartbroken as I had been when I said goodbye to Batistuta. I must've sensed that God was preparing me for the joy of 2022 when I watched alone in the basement, far from Nono, Mrs. Squittieri, and PS 14, as Argentina earned its third star. At the Lusail Stadium after the final whistle blew, Batistuta was crying again—though this time joyously, in the stands, surrounded by former teammates who had suffered elimination with him two decades earlier.

As time passes, I cannot help but think of Batistuta as often as I flip open my laptop. His name still appears in most of my passwords. And when I click the channel over to a soccer game, I see him in every stone-footed striker galloping into the penalty area to crash into a cross or an opponent. Even women's soccer players. I loved Abby Wambach because I first loved Batistuta. And I expect it to be this way even as my heroes are replaced by the people in my life who meet my adult longings the way Batistuta did my childhood ones. I imagine that one day my daughter, Alba, will hear my stories of Batistuta and ask me, "Daddy, is that like Mal Swanson for me?" or "You mean like Rose Lavelle? She scores some pretty cool goals." And I'll say: "Yes, sweetheart—exactly. Just like them."

I'll Never Be a Frontiersman

E very time I feel uncomfortable or suffer some slight inconvenience—when the water in the shower takes too long to heat or the internet crashes in the middle of my favorite Netflix show—I try to think about taking a dump in the woods.

Take a minute and try it for yourself. Picture the time you drove to Target with your children screaming in the back seat and, just as you turned into the parking lot, a teenager blowing vape smoke from the window of an oversized pickup truck cut you off. The vital seconds lost were just enough for another teenager—this one blaring mumble rap from the blown-out speakers of a rundown sports car—to snatch the last spot closest to the entrance. Or the time you got on an airplane and it looked like you might have an entire row to yourself until the final person to board took the seat right beside you. Or when your laptop updated for an hour before crashing, you tore a hole in the crotch of your pants in the middle of the workday, or you forgot the PIN to your debit card and got locked out of your bank account. Insert any of your most recent inconveniences. Now think about taking a dump in the woods. All better?

This revelation came to me in the shower on a Friday morning in September 2021. The night before, I had gone up alone to the tiny house my father-in-law fixed up just outside Stardust Marina on Norris Lake. For a few years, he and I have been working on a still-unfinished memoir about fatherhood. When I was busy with my day job and zapped of energy as I waited for my son, Enzo, to be born, he offered me the place, whenever I wanted, to isolate and write in. Out there, I would have no WiFi or cell phone reception to distract me. I left home with only my laptop to write in and a copy of *The Catcher in the Rye* for when I needed a break from thinking or typing.

As I massaged shampoo into my hair, I wondered why I hadn't disconnected before. Why hadn't I dropped everything and taken a long weekend to write in isolation, without texts, emails, and phone calls interrupting me every five minutes—with even social media out of reach? After getting out of the shower, I put on some clothes and walked onto the front porch, where I could hear the leaves shaking in the wind and see the bluegill swimming peacefully beside the dock. That's when the thought suddenly hit me: *If you had lived a hundred years ago, imagine all the books you would've written.*

Just seconds later, a second thought hit me—of having to take a dump in the woods.

I've often imagined myself as a beef-eating gaucho of the Argentinian pampas or a cowboy in a Colter Wall song. My dad, who grew up in the fertile grasslands of Santa Fe and Buenos Aires provinces, placed a fishing pole in my hand when I was still in diapers and taught me how to use a shotgun to take down doves and rabbits before I turned 10. In third grade, I joined the Boy Scouts and went on camping trips to West Jersey, where city kids could explore the woods and learn to throw axes and start fires without matches. On one of those trips, a boy in my troop named Ricardo felt a pang in his gut and dropped his trousers. He was beside a tree less than a hundred yards from our cabin. After he had finished, another boy came up behind and spooked him. Ricardo tripped and fell hand-first into his poop. I've pictured Ricardo's horrified reaction in all the woods I've been in since. And when the urge has come, I've held it.

When I went with Mickey and Jeremy, my childhood best friends, to the Adirondack Mountains in upstate New York weeks before leaving for college, I brought a handheld plastic shovel. I bought it at Campor, an outdoor store in the suburbs where we had stopped days before to buy all kinds of gear, including ropes for hanging our food out of the reach of black bears and a tent that we slept in the two nights we spent on either side of Pharaoh Mountain. Jeremy had read a guideline saying campers who needed to poop were expected to dig a hole in the dirt, deposit their turds into it, then cover it back over. I imagined a real man, after taking his dump, would rip leaves from the closest tree and use that to clean himself. And then, before I got in the car, I realized I had no idea what poison ivy looks like. So I tossed a pack of baby wipes into my bag.

I escape into books like *A Walk in the Woods, Blue Highways,* and *Into Thin Air* to reconnect with the past me who believed there were great adventures out there I'd be brave enough to take. But in real life, my experiences with isolation have been few and far between. I've never wandered more than a couple of hours' walk from cellphone reception or the touch of another human being. In the tiny home beside the lake, I wrote from a mattress in the loft, above a refrigerator and microwave I used to warm up food my wife, Haley, had packed me the night before. The home was insulated. There was a working toilet, two-ply toilet paper, and peanut M&Ms, which my mother-in-law keeps stocked in the snack drawer because she knows they're my favorite.

Even though we take pictures of excursions into the woods or moments spent wading through water in a mountain stream and post them to Instagram with captions like "Escaping for a while," who are we kidding? Isolation isn't kicking off your flip-flops in a temperature-controlled house or driving your Subaru into a state park for the night. It's taking baths in cold lake water and dumps beside a tree in the forest, wiping your butt with dried leaves, then shoveling dirt over the turd as you gag from the fumes. It's figuring out what berries to eat and which will kill you like Chris McCandless in *Into the Wild.*

The campus of William Paterson University, where I went to college, is nestled between the frenzied concrete maze that is Paterson, New Jersey, and the largest tract of uninterrupted forest in the northern part of the state. During freshman year biology, our professor walked us through those woods to a waterfall and then up to the bald summit of High Mountain, where you can peer through the smog and make out the Manhattan skyline. I can't remember the names of the tree species we learned about that semester, but I do remember something that my campus minister, Ken Van Der Wall—a tall, bald Dutchman who'd left western Michigan in the 1970s to minister to coastal heathens—told us. Pastor Ken said religious people in America tend to major in the minors of life. We get so wrapped up in whether someone takes off their hat for the national anthem or memorizes a string of Bible verses that we forget to draw pictures with the children of prisoners or share meals with the poor.

I major in the trivial. I get my feet stuck in the mud, focusing on life's minutiae, not the bigger picture. Every day, I fight a losing battle against my dwindling attention span and the millions of distractions it turns to that aren't the things I say I really care about. Most days, it's hardly a fight; I give in before I get out from under the bedsheets.

In my early 20s, when I still harbored dreams of trotting the globe, I watched a lot of YouTube videos. Those were the early days of the platform, before advertisers and influencers, when one of the most popular creators on the site was a guy named Matt who shot videos of himself dancing with strangers in beautiful places around the world. Around that time, Jeremy introduced me to TED Talks, which I consumed like teenagers today watching TikTok. I remember a talk from the writer A. J. Jacobs, who spent a year living according to the rules of the Old Testament. He couldn't shave his beard or sit where a menstruating woman had sat on the subway. He couldn't wear cotton blend fabrics. Every day he had embarrassing conversations. Most nights, he felt like a fool or worse. But in the end, he had learned a few lessons. One of them was to be grateful. "My behavior changed my thoughts," he said. "I started to change my perspective to realize the hundreds of little things that go right in my life every day that I was taking for granted instead of the few things that go wrong."

Before I spent a night alone at the tiny home, my most pressing source of anxiety was my car. Somehow, I had averaged nearly one flat tire a week for a month. Even the guys at Fisher Tire couldn't believe how adept I was at finding a nail in the road to drive over. In my daydreams of living inside a folk song, there are no motor vehicles or stagecoaches. But in real life, I depend on my Honda Civic from daybreak to sunset. "In the South, we drive everywhere," Haley explains when I question why she's getting in the car to go from one end of the shopping center to the other, a total distance of .01 miles.

I'm terrified of breaking down and being left stranded on the side of the highway. On long car trips, I breathe easy only during the first and last hundred miles, when I'm close enough to home or my destination that if the brakes were to fail or the car explode a AAA tow truck would pick me up without charging extra. During the month I spent afflicted with flat tires, I read a book about stoicism that a friend lent me. And even though I'm no good at focusing my energy on the things that I can control over what I can't, I did start to feel grateful for the days when I get up, turn on the car, and there isn't a sensor lit up on the dashboard.

I'm sure I will continue to struggle with the tension of gratitude, just as I do with the tension of living the life I have versus the one I imagined for myself as a kid. I'm striving to be grateful for the many ways I'm comfortable. To stop moaning about each inconvenience or hurdle—whether it's a teenager in a loud car keeping me from getting a good parking spot at Target or a Monday morning filled with emails instead of staring past my coffee into a body of water full of fish I could be catching.

So the next time a Spotify playlist won't load because my phone insists on trying to connect to WiFi in the middle of Interstate 40 or my air conditioning starts acting up, I'm not going to lock myself in the closet and declare the day a failure. When I find a hole in my favorite soccer jersey or bust my taillight backing into the garbage can the neighbor left out in the alleyway, I will remind myself of this: at least I've got toilet paper.

Trout Fishing in Arkansas

The solution to any problem—work, love, money, whatever—is to go fishing, and the worse the problem, the longer the trip should be.

—John Gierach, *Standing in a River Waving a Stick*

Of course Derrick had to be the one to do it, because that's what guys who are saved in people's phones as The Fish Whisperer do: they catch big fish. And not just big ones. They catch the biggest ones. And what's worse is that they hate to do it; they apologize for doing it. But as the April light dimmed over Arkansas, he just couldn't help himself.

Knee-deep in the water on the last night of a five-day trip to the Spring River, we were casting our fly rods in search of monsters to hook when Derrick shouted, "Fish!" I turned my head just in time to see his rod tip bend so violently that I thought a cinder block had wrapped around the end of his line. After a good fight, Derrick wrestled a gluttonous rainbow trout to shore. It was big—perhaps big enough to surpass the trip's largest catch, a 20-inch rainbow I had pulled into our guide's boat the afternoon before.

Jonathan rushed over and pulled out his measuring tape. "He's got you beat, Jersey!" he announced as we stood around gawking at the two-foot marker. I didn't take more than a glance at the black line on the tape before shifting my gaze to the man in the straw hat: a 53-year-old Zen master in prescription glasses who fished a magical fly he named after himself. "Sorry, Jersey," he said, smiling wide and grabbing the fish around its meaty back to pose for a victory photo.

The trip to Arkansas was my first time venturing from home with a group of men whose sole intention was to catch trout. Besides the Fish Whisperer and me, our crew consisted of Kohl, a filmmaker, and Jonathan, who served unofficially as my trout sensei after introducing me to fly fishing only a year and a half earlier. Before we left, Jonathan had contacted Mark Crawford, the sole fly fishing guide in that part of Arkansas, and hired him and his son, Hunter, to lead us on the second and third days of the trip. For the first and final days, we'd fish alone on a stretch of water in front of our cabin, just a mile downriver from the dam.

The cabin's owner was a middle-aged man known locally as Busch Kurt. The afternoon he welcomed us, Kurt showed up with a can of Busch beer in his hand, downed a second while making small talk, and cracked open a third, which he left full on the patio table—all inside the time it took me to rig up my rod and slide on my waders. Eager to get my line in the water, I speed-walked to the bank and trudged in. I hooked a smallmouth bass within a few casts; Busch Kurt, elated by my quick success, announced from the porch that he'd been stocking them for his guests. (Mark Crawford later told us that our host was actually catching bass downriver, transporting them in his pickup truck, and tossing them in the water in front of the cabin.)

When I told a friend who grew up in Arkansas that I was heading to fish the Spring River, he asked if I was really going for the trout or if I had come up with a clever excuse for attending one of the many topless summer boat parties hosted by DJ Supermoon. Anyone who drives through Mammoth Springs, Arkansas (population: 935) will recognize the 50-year-old Speedo-clad cowboy whose face adorns approximately 75 percent of the sign welcoming you to town. But we weren't there for Mardi Gras. We were there to take our shot at some of the state's finest trout in a place most sober folks had never heard of.

On the morning of our departure, we piled into Kohl's truck and rode eight hours west from Knoxville, talking fly selection and daydreaming about how many trout we'd each catch: 50, 60, maybe even 100 over the course of the trip. The numbers were preposterous for me. Even though I had grown up fishing with my dad in New Jersey, I was a worm and minnow guy until Sensei Jon, as I'd come to call Jonathan, persuaded me to hang up my spin rod and bury my nightcrawlers in the dirt. "There's no art in throwing doughballs or worms," he told me through cigar haze in his workshop late one night while flipping through pictures of enormous fish he'd caught on microscopic artificial flies. "Fly fishing is art. And aren't you supposed to be a writer?" Jonathan had successfully appealed to my snobbery, conjuring up images of Robert Redford's *A River Runs Through It*, which I'd seen on TV as a boy.

Over several trips to the Holston, Clinch, and Watauga rivers from July 2019 to May 2020, Sensei Jon taught me how to cast a fly rod, mend a line, and carefully fight a fish, not muscling it onto shore like I could with my spin rod. Twice, desperate to see me land a trout, he hooked into one then handed me the rod to let me fight it alone. Both times, I inevitably did something wrong and it broke me off. Fly fishing turned out to be as hard as it looks. After the eighth skunking in a row, I was deflated and defeated.

Then one morning in June, Jonathan invited me to fish a small stream in Townsend that flows into the Little River of the Great Smoky Mountains. That's where I learned to use a Japanese cane pole called a tenkara rod. In the midst of the pandemic, I took every chance I got to escape into the mountains. I netted at least a dozen or more trout on two or three occasions. But they were all wild brookies and rainbows under 10 inches long. I'd yet to hook into the kinds of monsters that live beneath the surface of the Spring River.

Things were off to a good start at Busch Kurt's. We fished until sundown, each member of our party claiming a sliver of a 200-yard section of river and netting at least one sizable rainbow trout. Then we returned to the porch, gorged ourselves on T-bone steaks Jonathan grilled on the fire pit, and packed tobacco pipes while making plans of attack based on what God and the river had revealed to us that afternoon.

Each morning, we woke up with the sun and cast our lines straight into the water. Light beer, beef jerky, and trail mix fueled us. And whether with Mark or learning from each other (though mainly from Derrick), we pulled in all kinds of trout—from the skinny to the engorged, the recently stocked to the well-aged, some mushy and pale, others radiant and robust. Each one we carefully unhooked and tossed back into the water to live another day.

Resting on the bank, looking back over the photos of our best catches, we wondered why so few others had come from as far away as we had. Before the trip, I'd run some Google searches and couldn't find a single article in a prominent fly-fishing magazine about the Spring River and the wonders Mark Crawford had shown us. Having grown up in Mammoth Springs and fished the river with his grandfather, he knew it better than anyone. After finishing school, he worked in factories until his first wife left him with Hunter, then just two years old. To turn his attention away from his daily worries, Mark learned to tie artificial trout flies. Eventually people started buying his patterns, which trout went out of their way to chase down, and he went on to earn a reputation for taking people out into his put-and-take fishery to catch and release trout as they do in Colorado and Wyoming.

While eating ham-and-cheese sandwiches during our first float, he told us about his plans to turn the river into a premier trout fishing destination rivaling the White and Little Red. He was already in contact with national conservation groups. Besides having a killer sense of humor and hands that'll tie on a new fly as fast as a Wild West sharpshooter, Mark makes you feel like a friend when you're in his boat, even if you're only there as half of a business transaction.

By the end of our trip, I hadn't caught anywhere near the number of trout I had imagined on our drive west. Derrick might've caught a hundred trout over five days. Jonathan got close, topping 80. I may have netted 40 (though I'll claim every fish that broke off my fly or freed himself as I reeled him into my waiting net). The good news is that I did at least manage a consolation prize, which I accepted begrudgingly, for catching the most diverse species of fish: a creek chub, shiner, smallmouth, rock bass, long-ear sunfish, and other species that weren't monstrous salmonids. I guess you can take that, Fish Whisperer.

Before heading to Arkansas, I had planned on taking meticulous notes and recording conversations and dispatches on my iPhone for an essay I'd write and pitch to an outdoor magazine once I got home. I was going to be the first writer to put a spotlight on the Spring River. More importantly, I was going to show the world that I had chops as a chronicler of outdoor adventures.

On the morning of our first float with Mark, he welcomed us to the ramshackle fly shop he and his friends had built by hand. His plan for the day was simple: leading us into trout-rich water, where we'd take so many photos holding large fish that our Instagram follower numbers would skyrocket. He'd then feed us a lunch of roasted groundhog. If we were lucky, we might even find Sasquatch hiding in the bush (the closest we got was another half-naked photo of DJ Supermoon on a sign in front of his riverside mansion). As Mark rowed us out to the first fishable section of the river, I asked about his background and what had led him to a life of guiding tourists, most with no idea what they were doing, to catch trout. I spoke his responses as notes into my phone.

But it wasn't long before I closed my recorder app and lost my gaze in the tree line. Had I gone to Arkansas to work? Was I probing Mark with questions because I was genuinely curious about his story or because I wanted to create a caricature that might make readers laugh? As much as I wanted to write some beautiful 5,000-word essay to share with anglers across America, the more time I spent on the water with Mark and my friends, the more that urge to write something elegant and celebrated disappeared—as most things do when you're fly fishing.

When there's a fly you've painstakingly tied using elk hair, pheasant tail, wire, and thread floating just above or below the water's surface, losing focus for even a split second might result in a missed strike. "A trout can spit out a fly in one one-hundredth of a second," the Fish Whisperer told us, sharing his ancient wisdom. "Sometimes even faster." If you do manage to hook one, too much tension on the line or a bad slip on the river bottom that leaves you fully submerged and 20 yards downstream will also result in a lost fish. Focus is essential to success in this game.

But there's also the solace of fishing: the cool water splashes against your waders, vapor rises from the water, bald eagles fly overhead and nest in a tree 30 yards above you. The sun rises and falls. But above all, there is friendship: a sense of brotherhood with guys who had once been strangers but with whom I've now written a real-life story that I'll retell for as long as I've got my head on straight.

Moving into the middle stage of my life—married with young children, a mortgage, debts to pay, a career to grow—the opportunities I'll have to string together days of fishing with my friends are whittling down. When Jonathan first suggested the Arkansas trip during one of our weekly fly-tying nights, I didn't think I'd go. I had a young daughter, responsibilities, and no disposable income. But Haley's willingness to be a single parent for five days, and Jonathan's leadership over every logistical aspect of our preparation, pushed the obstacles from my path. And because of that, I wasn't left on the sofa folding underwear, jealously looking at pictures of fish on Instagram. I could marvel in real life at the wonder of a fish glistening inside my net.

Calling this type of trip an escape isn't entirely accurate. I didn't need to escape. I needed to be plugged back into the electrical socket, charging life into my ever-draining battery. We all need that sometimes, whether it's meditating in a yoga class, listening to music on an old record player, joining a pickleball league, or simply spending time on the water with close friends, focused entirely on something that isn't those things that consume the other hours of our lives.

A year after that April in Arkansas, my son, Enzo, was born. Jonathan had a son, too. Kohl was off somewhere in Europe, riding a motorcycle and taking pictures. The Fish Whisperer was another year older, another year wiser, and still pulling monsters out of whatever stream, river, pond, ocean, glacial lake, or roadside puddle he chose to fish. We haven't returned to the Spring River. I have no idea if we ever will. But I hope we do. And even if we don't, I'll have the stories and images of that one trip, not published in some fancy outdoor magazine but saved permanently in my memory bank.

The Joy of Reading

I have always imagined that Paradise will be a kind of library.

—Jorge Luis Borges

Whenever I wander through a used bookstore anywhere in the world, I like to pick up an old paperback—a grimy one with a torn-up cover and pencil marks on the pages—and picture not the last, but maybe the tenth-to-last person to hold it in their hands. I picture where it lived before it got there: perhaps on another shelf hundreds or thousands of miles away. Sometimes, on the spine, I'll find a sticker from a library it once belonged to in a different state. I hadn't noticed this until the early months of the pandemic, when Knoxville's iconic warehouse-sized bookstore McKay's closed indefinitely and I had to resort to ordering books online. They arrived from libraries in Phoenix, San Francisco, and Las Cruces. Why they had been marked for departure, I'll never know.

"Where was home before it was here?" I ask myself while meandering for hours through the mazy aisles, combing through books with long-forgotten dedications inside the front cover and the occasional handwritten note used as a bookmark by owners who forgot it was there.

On Saturday afternoons when it's rainy and cold, or I don't have time or energy for much else, I walk the bookstore like a kid exploring the woods behind their parents' house. I flip over rocks and look for mysteries. I murmur to myself, with music in my headphones and a list of books on my cell phone. Few things compare to the dopamine spike of coming upon books from that list on a dusty shelf, knowing how much easier it would've been to order them through Amazon.

As a boy, I wasn't an obsessive reader. I was barely a reader at all. My hometown of Bayonne, New Jersey, has a single public library, and I didn't spend much time there. (The first bookstore I remember walking into was a Barnes & Noble in college.) I did get issues of *Highlights* and *Nat Geo Kids* ordered to the house as a boy. This past summer, my brother found a link to an eBay page selling wildlife fact files from the 1990s that I remember my mom buying (from where I have no clue) because I liked looking at the pictures of cheetahs in the Serengeti. We owned a few novels, too—*Frankenstein*, *Tom Sawyer*. In the days before handheld computer phones, I flipped through my dad's fishing magazines and thick texts about coins and Argentinian history that Nono kept in the living room of his apartment, just downstairs from my parents.

My relationship with reading is a slow-burn love affair that ignited during my junior year at Bayonne High School. Mr. Prezioso and Mr. Sweeney, a grumpy pair of old-timey teachers who taught the dual English–history honors course, introduced me to the great works of literature that remain among my favorites: *The Great Gatsby*; *Winesburg, Ohio*; *Death of a Salesman*; and *The Sun Also Rises*. Learning about the Lost Generation writers toiling away in Paris bars in the 1920s made me envious that I hadn't been there lingering in the dark beside them. The feeling mirrors the not-quite nostalgia I experience to this day when listening to Nono tell stories of his childhood in Argentina. It's a time-bending longing, like the kind Argentine writer Jorge Luis Borges describes in his 1981 poem "Nostalgia del presente," which I translated to English:

> *In that precise moment he said to himself: What would I not give for the joy of being at your side in Iceland under the grand unmoving day and to partake of the now, as one partakes of music or the taste of fruit. At that precise moment, he was together with her in Iceland.*

When I open a book that once belonged to someone else, I travel across space and time. I become the astronaut Joseph Cooper (played by Matthew McConaughey) in *Interstellar*, watching from behind the bookcase as a stranger sniffles at the same lines in the same books that now fill the shelves of my office library. I struggle to describe it, just as I've struggled for years to articulate to Haley why my books should be out in the open and not hidden away in the basement. "When a new friend sees I own a copy of No Country for Old Men, they'll want to debate with me about whether I thought the book or film was better—it's a conversation starter," I say, as she keeps her index finger firmly pointed toward the stairs, unconvinced by my appeal to her artistic sensibility.

Since high school, my favorite novel has been J. D. Salinger's The Catcher in the Rye. I've reread it five or six times and keep giveaway copies for friends. The book is more than 70 years old; its protagonist, Holden Caulfield, is less than half the age I am today. Yet I find so much of myself in it. There are moments in the novel when Caulfield addresses the reader directly, saying things I've said or could say. Remembering a visit to the Museum of Natural History, he muses:

> The best thing . . . in that museum was that everything always stayed right where it was. You could go there a hundred thousand times, and that Eskimo would still be just finished catching those two fish, the birds would still be on their way south, the deers would still be drinking out of that water hole, with their pretty antlers and their pretty, skinny legs. . . . The only thing that would be different would be you. Not that you'd be so much older or anything. It wouldn't be that, exactly. You'd just be different, that's all. You'd have an overcoat this time. Or the

> *kid that was your partner in line the last time had got*
> *scarlet fever and you'd have a new partner. Or you'd*
> *have a substitute taking the class, instead of Miss*
> *Aigletinger. Or you'd heard your mother and father*
> *having a terrific fight in the bathroom. Or you'd just*
> *passed by one of those puddles in the street with*
> *gasoline rainbows in them. I mean you'd be different*
> *in some way—I can't explain what I mean.*

Like all great art, books have this magical ability to connect you to a fictional character living in a time and place you'll never visit (at least until Mark Zuckerberg and Tim Cook figure out how to configure virtual reality headsets with time travel features). Tying my own story in with the one I'm reading is how I often judge art's true value. *Is there a lesson for me to take from this?* Books aren't so much an escape into a fabricated paradise or hellscape. At their core, Kazuo Ishiguro's *Never Let Me Go*, Philip Dick's *Do Androids Dream of Electric Sheep?*, Cormac McCarthy's *The Road*, and others like them are portals to alternate universes in which you are still human—where the existential struggle of carving out purpose and finding direction amidst the chaos is as tangible as when you're sitting on the couch debating whether you should go back to school, buy a ring, try for a baby, or leave home and not come back.

In the movie version of one of my favorite books, *The Motorcycle Diaries*, a young Che Guevara (played by Mexican actor Gael Garcia Bernal) is on a road trip across South

America with his best friend. At the ruins of Machu Picchu, he asks, "How is it possible to feel nostalgia for a world you never knew?" The answer is not clear to me. But I know I've felt it. With an open book in my hands, I've transformed, like Borges, into a time-traveling stranger in Iceland, a crime-fighting detective like Sherlock Holmes, a misunderstood war veteran like Billy Pilgrim in *Slaughterhouse-Five*, a whiskey-drunk writer like Hemingway or Fitzgerald, and countless other versions of myself that may exist in the multiverse of roads not traveled. But how could I ever be those things?

My dad once told me that when we read about war as boys, we all imagine ourselves as the man with the sniper rifle hiding in the trees and not the first one felled by bullets, stones, or swords. Still, it doesn't hurt to imagine. The best books have inspired me to become more than who I am at this very moment. They've inspired me to be a more welcoming neighbor, a more affectionate husband, a kinder friend and braver and more compassionate human being—to be wise, strong, sensitive, curious, and unwilling to pack it in when times get tough.

And if the world is to end, and I get just a few hours left on Earth and a few possessions to carry into alien captivity (or whatever future comes next), you'll know exactly where to find me: wandering one last time through a used bookstore searching for buried treasure.

Field of Dreams

You know, we just don't recognize the most significant moments of our lives while they're happening. Back then I thought, "Well, there'll be other days." I didn't realize that that was the only day.

—Dr. Archibald "Moonlight" Graham, *Field of Dreams*

Three or four nights a week, I'd meet them at 16th Street Park to kick around a soccer ball. It was our ritual—men, young and old, known only by our nicknames: Chombi, Chele, Lupe, Guanaco, Jamón. And me, Batistuta.

The games were *picaditos*: informal gatherings of construction and white-collar workers, high school students, servers and line cooks—almost all immigrants or sons of immigrants. We arrived at the patchy grass field around 6:30 every night with our fingers crossed, all hoping that we'd be the ones to pull off a nutmeg or *rabona* and avoid being embarrassed by the few players who had played professionally in Honduras or Colombia before coming north.

We played 5-v-4 or 9-v-8 or 12-v-12 in the outfields of baseball diamonds, where there were no sidelines or out-of-bounds. The goalposts were two backpacks or pairs of sneakers and sweaters balled up and placed five paces apart. The teams were picked by veterans like *El Viejo* (The Old Man), who waited around beside the goals until the better players showed up so he could pick them for his team. His salad days long gone, he'd enjoy a brief return to glory by teaming up with young headliners like *Tarzán*, a long-haired Honduran who spoke like a Puerto Rican and broke ankles without ever touching the ball, and JP, an equally slick-footed Ecuadorian who was always decked out in a fresh kit from one of his favorite European club teams.

But everything changed on Sundays, when a veteran Ecuadorian named Armando—who we all knew as Rossi because of the Paolo Rossi Italy jersey he wore—showed up with two small training goals. His arrival brought a civility that was otherwise missing as players toed the line between toying with opponents and provoking them with a slight that could result in a retaliatory forearm across the jaw. When Rossi and *El Hombre de Hierro* (Iron Man), a 68-year-old who remains the measure for how long I hope to play this magical game, showed up with their crew of mostly older Jehovah Witnesses, everyone was on their best behavior. And the best news for me and my friends, who were usually the worst of quietest or most American guys on the field, was that Rossi always picked us for his team.

Once the ball was kicked, Rossi would shout some variation of *Los buenos contra los malos* and, when we'd go down a goal or two, *Van perdiendo los buenos*—rituals I picked up on and repeat on the fields of Knoxville many years later. He kept the atmosphere light, gently ribbing players for missing a shot on one of his 6x4 goals, which everyone knew he'd take down and leave with if you misbehaved. One winter night, when the cold had frozen over the muddy field, we all drove out to an indoor facility in the suburbs. Halfway through the game, Tarzán was fouled hard by another Central American. They pummeled each other with fists until we could break up the fight. Since the goals were cut into the facility's walls, Rossi couldn't pack them into a bag and carry them to his car. So he took the ball away and sat everyone down on the bench, lecturing us like a schoolteacher who had caught his students shooting spitballs while his back was turned. The guilty parties embraced and pleaded with Rossi to continue playing. But he instructed everyone to go home and think about what they had done—which was easy for me and my friends to do, since we were riding in Rossi's car.

From the time I was 14 until I left Bayonne eight years later, I spent hundreds of hours of my life kicking a ball around with these guys. Most of them were Hispanic laborers. Some, like Guanaco, whose real name I cannot remember for my life, were high school students who would later become laborers. (A guanaco is a species of South American camel; I also cannot tell you why people from El Salvador are identified using that term.)

I'll never forget, in college, waking up early on a Saturday morning and stopping in a nearby Exxon with my dad before going with him to a plumbing job in the suburbs. I ran into Guanaco in the snack aisle, where I'd gone to grab one of those Bon Appétit danishes sold in every gas station in America. "*Que hacés por acá hermano?*" I asked him. He told me he worked at the port, his eyes red from lack of sleep. That was the first time it hit me: once I graduated, I'd leave behind blue-collar work—probably even Bayonne—forever. But many of those guys, who were paperless and not fluent in English, were stuck working manual labor jobs they clocked in at before sunrise. Their escape came at night, playing pickup soccer at the park.

It wasn't only Hispanic immigrants who showed up. There was a mixed bag of other characters, including Mohammed, an Egyptian computer science professor who drove golf balls he carried in a plastic shopping bag around the field until game time, and Robert Borowski, a Polish kid I'd played travel soccer with, whose dad taught us the proper technique for injuring an opponent's knee from behind when we were 10 years old. I never thought about it then, but rarely were there any women. Those who did come were there not to play but to verify that their husbands had not lied about going to the field and gone to the bar instead. They walked laps on the concrete track that circled the fields while their kids entertained each other behind the goals. I wish I could travel back in time with Haley, a ponytailed white girl whose mouth, as much as her skills, would've left the guys astounded, as if an alien had just strapped on a pair of cleats.

There is something I dearly miss about the freedom I experienced playing pickup at 16th Street, where time wasn't kept and there were no yellow cards or VAR checks. When the ball was blasted from our pitiful patch of grass onto the red-dirt baseball diamond 20 yards away, someone would retrieve it and dribble in 20 yards alone—no throw-ins or set pieces. There were audacious moves attempted over and over that even Zidane could not pull off in a competitive game. Out there on the field of dreams, it didn't matter if you'd missed a bicycle kick or a rainbow a dozen times if you pulled it off just once. Because scores weren't calculated based on who put the most goals in the back of the net but who managed something they could brag about every night for the next week as everyone changed into their jerseys. Once Guanaco, who had a sublime touch and a knack for the unpredictable, rainbowed the ball over my head as I went to tackle him. I did the only acceptable thing, applying the lesson Nono had taught me: if the ball gets past you, the player mustn't. I chopped at his knees with the fury of an axe striking a cypress tree, and he fell to the ground like Cristiano Ronaldo. "*No seas payaso que acá no hay arbitro,*" I said with a snicker. He was on his feet quicker than a lightning strike. An inch from my face, he shouted what he'd do to me if we were back in El Salvador. Rather than trading punches, we'd go on to combine for many goals in the years before I moved away.

When I was a teenager, an unbelievable thing happened. On a rare summer night when the city had left the full-sized soccer goals out after a youth scrimmage that afternoon, an informal game took shape on the big field. Mexicans and Egyptians lined up on each half, all wearing counterfeit jerseys from their national teams and preparing to face off in an intercontinental battle. I still remember the Egyptian goal celebrations: one player pretending to shine another's shoes, another grinning like Mohamed Salah and posing for a picture in front of an imaginary camera. The Mexicans, many of whom had Corona bellies that leaked out from the bottom of their jerseys, won 9–3.

But it wasn't just them. Every night we were all out there representing our national pride. It didn't matter if you were from Nicaragua, Nigeria, or New Zealand, you knew better than to show up wearing your team's jersey after an embarrassing loss. When Argentina would get eliminated from a World Cup or a Copa América, I was always left with an impossible choice: staying home and licking my wounds or showing up just to hear Viejo and JP roasting me, as creatively as possible, from 50 yards away as soon as they caught sight of my sky blue jersey.

Despite all the time I spent out there, I wasn't, and am still not, a great soccer player. My dad, who played in the reserve side of a professional team in Argentina, had tried his best to transmit his abilities to his firstborn son. Before I was old enough to play regularly with grown men, he'd take me after work to the field and teach me how to hit the ball with the outside of my foot and how to place a shot within a five-inch radius of the top corner. But I could never figure out how to play like a real Argentinean. My feet were like two boulders. My legs so stiff that I couldn't dribble 10 feet without tripping over the ball. I had no waist—no *cintura,* as Nono says. But that didn't matter. The men I played with still called me by the name of my hero.

In the late 2000s, another Argentinian emerged as the most famous soccer player in the world. One day a trio of Cubans hopped the yellow brick wall and took the dirt trail to the fields. The leader of the troupe, after hearing my accent, screamed, "Messi!" (It wasn't—it still isn't—uncommon when meeting immigrants, whether Uruguayan or Macedonian, that the first thing I also say, after they reveal where they're from, is the name of a very famous soccer player from that country: "Forlán!" "Pandev!") The others quickly corrected the newcomer: *No, ese es Batistuta, amigo.*

More than a decade has passed since anyone on a soccer field has called me by my hero's name. During my first weeks in Knoxville in 2011, I drove to local parks seeking out foreigners kicking soccer balls in the grass. But I rarely found any. Then a co-worker invited me to play on Wednesday nights at an indoor facility called D1, and I realized that in places like Knoxville—far from the concrete immigrant hubs I'd known before—soccer is organized. If you want to play, you've got to pay, regardless of whether you're a toddler or an old-timer on Social Security. So you can imagine my relief when someone told me about the Chinese grad students who played on Saturday mornings at the university rec center and the Brazilians who got together on the other side of town at Cool Sports.

My favorite place to play pickup in Knoxville, though, was the overgrown field at Liberty Street, where you'd see Koreans, Arabs, and Russians smoking cigarettes outside their cars before dribbling circles around players half their age. That sent me back in time to the days at 16th Street when a bunch of guys who didn't care to know your real name, your place of employment, or your marital status would talk for days about a ridiculous goal you scored to end a game. "You see the backheel *ese mamahuevo* tried last week?" somebody would ask, bellowing as flocks of us gathered to shoot the bull before the start of the next pickup. "He thinks he's Ronaldinho!"

Hours later, with no Rossi around to mediate, somebody would get fed up with the insults or the roughhousing, snatch up their sneakers and hoodie from the goal, and head home, leaving one of the makeshift posts lopsided for the last hour of play. How I miss the arguments about whether a shot had been kicked too high above a backpack to count! Or when, after calling it a night, we'd sit huddled in the grass for an hour or two, talking about our favorite players and teams from Europe and South America, learning a little about each other's lives away from the football pitch.

For years, especially when my best friends were away at college, and I was a stone's throw from those fields, trying to figure out where my road in life would lead, the soccer community at 16th Street meant everything to me. And I recognize we couldn't recreate it now. But if I had the keys to a time machine, I know I wouldn't hesitate to return, for a single night, to play soccer with those ruffians one last time.

Dispatches to My Children

Words have a longevity I do not.

—Paul Kalanithi, *When Breathe Becomes Air*

It was 5 a.m., and despite the darkness that enveloped the room, I knew immediately after opening my eyes there wasn't a chance I was going to fall back asleep.

It's not uncommon for me to wake up hours before the alarm sounds, unsure whether to try nodding back off or staying up, brewing coffee, and getting an early start to the day like podcast-hosting entrepreneurs and Mark Wahlberg tell us to. Usually I've got a song lyric trapped in my head or an image from a dream that kick-starts a slideshow of memories from childhood. But there are mornings when I experience a feeling bordering on epiphany, like a light bulb that clicks on after a blackout. I scramble to write these down in the notes app on my phone, afraid that if I don't immediately try to remember them they'll vanish into the black pit, lost forever. And that's what must have happened that morning.

The dead man came to me as an apparition. I'm not sure why; we weren't close, more acquaintances than friends. We attended the same church for years, seeing each other at Sunday services and other events and speaking a few words here or there. The month Alba was born—it was so early in the pandemic that wearing a mask hadn't become a political statement yet—I ran into his wife outside Aldi while returning the cart so I could salvage my quarter. We stood on the curb discussing the lockdown, having babies, and small groups at church. I drove home and told Haley about it as we put away the groceries. "Maybe now that we're parents, we could be friends with them," I said. Because new parents always think about who they can be friends with since they can no longer stay out past 7:30 p.m. or drink more than two glasses of wine without getting a headache.

A year and a half later, he was gone. I learned from the obituary that he was younger than me. I already knew that he was smarter—he was a doctor—and in better physical shape. He died suddenly of complications from a rare disease. And though I didn't know him well, I grieved. I thought of his wife that day outside of Aldi. I thought of their two kids. Then I thought of what it might be like to die and leave behind my family.

I ran the numbers in my head, reassuring myself that it was impossible. And yet, since his death I wake up each morning with the fear of dying fresh on my mind. When I pray in the car on my drive to the gym or work, the first words I utter are some version of, "Thank you, God, for filling my lungs with air today." And it's not because I'm pious. It's because I'm terrified. Before turning the key in the ignition, I've already imagined a dozen ways I might perish: being flattened by a texting teenager's pick-up truck while turning left on Broadway, slipping and falling from the railing of a cruise ship, getting locked in my body after foot surgery then buried alive after a nurse forgets to check if I'm really dead. The most frequent of these fears is being diagnosed with some incurable, only-detectable-when-it's-already-too-late disease, like a stage 4 cancer.

It is terrible to consider dying this young. It's also a testament to my cognitive dissonance. On the one hand, I think a mosquito bite that turns my skin too red is a sign I've contracted a flesh-eating virus. Then, once I've calmed down, I imagine the lives my children will choose and the Caribbean resorts where Haley and I will vacation once they're out of the house, the mortgage is paid off, and I can sit in a brown recliner with a horde of grandkids at my feet begging to hear my stories just as I begged Nono for his.

Because my children are so young, this is the awful truth: If I were to die today, the odds are they wouldn't remember the sound of my car pulling up in the driveway, seeing me walk through the door, feeling my arms wrap around them and my kiss land on their foreheads. All they would have are pictures and stories from their mother and Facebook posts family and friends write on the anniversary of my death. They would know the sound of my voice only through video, not because they remember hearing me whisper "I love you" in their ears before bed. When I think about it for too long I feel like a sling blade has just ripped right through my chest.

Before I was married or had children, my brother lent me a copy of Paul Kalanithi's memoir *When Breath Becomes Air*. Kalanithi, a writer and neurosurgeon, wrote the book while dying of lung cancer at 37—just three years older than I am today—in full knowledge that he'd leave behind a wife and a daughter too young to remember him. The physical act of reading that book and flipping through the pages as he chronicles the demise of their life together is devastating. His is not the only memoir written while the author is dying: computer science professor Randy Pausch wrote *The Last Lecture* and poet Nina Riggs *The Bright Hour* while succumbing to cancer. Both left behind spouses and children.

There must be something about knowing your life's expiration date is quickly approaching that inspires you to document as much of it as you can. I remember thinking as I read Kalanithi's memoir for the second time—just as I later thought when I learned of the man's death—that if I knew I were dying, I'd beg God for an extra day. I would spend those 24 hours writing letters and stories to my children. That way they would always know their dad and how much he loved them. I may die an old man, with my children and grandchildren at my bedside. But I may also die with the phantom sounds of a ticking clock in my ears: 24 months, 12, six, three, two, one. I may die unexpectedly, with no time to react or leave behind pieces of myself for my family.

I got out of bed with Haley still asleep and tiptoed into the office, where I opened a Google Doc. I titled it "Dispatches from Dad." Before the internet and livestream technology changed how we consume the news, dispatches were how we learned about wars, famines, and adventures in far-off places. From 1937 to 1939, Ernest Hemingway wrote them from the Spanish Civil War for newspapers in the United States. One of my favorite books, *The Lost City of Z*, initially published as a story in *The New Yorker* by David Grann, tells of explorer Percy Fawcett, who partly funded his travels to the Brazilian Amazon by writing dispatches for British newspapers. These field letters are meant to transport their readers to the exact time and place the writer experiences as they put pen to paper.

The running document is in a folder with all my other writing. At least twice a month, I add notes about what's happening in our family. Like anything chronicled before a significant moment that changes everything, they are unspectacular, covering the mundane occurrences of daily life, from work and play to potty training and childhood illness. When I'm in a pensive mood, I write about my longings for them and myself, my failures and regrets, which I hope they don't replicate. I share lighter anecdotes too, like when Alba learned to pray and thanked God for her stuffed bunny before her parents and when Enzo escaped the house through the doggie door.

Even though my dispatches are unremarkable, I imagine my children may one day cherish them as I do my parents' and grandparents' photo albums, which I rummage through every time I fly home to New Jersey. And while I find it curious how much attention we pay to letters not written for us, as Shaun Usher's *Letters of Note* anthologies prove, it doesn't matter if strangers' eyes ever see the words I write my children. They are literature for an audience of three. In the end, it may not even matter if I die before they can remember me, or if these letters become something they read out loud in their rooms or quietly under covers as they go off to college, fall in love, marry, and have children of their own. All I know—and I knew it immediately in the space between 5 and 5:01 a.m.—is that I should've never taken so long to start writing.

Jobs We Could Choose Instead

The waitress brought me another drink. She wanted to light my hurricane lamp again. I wouldn't let her. "Can you see anything in the dark with your sunglasses on?" she asked me. "The big show is inside my head," I said.

— Kurt Vonnegut, *Breakfast of Champions*

"There are only two types of jobs in the world," the Argentine writer Hernán Casciari says. "Those that existed back when we were still pure, and those that didn't." In Eden, there were cartoonists and cabinetmakers but no police or soccer referees. The noble professions—clown, baker, carpenter—are tethered to the most basic human needs. The others—politician, banker, and lawyer—emerged out of chaos and trickery, the consequence of humanity's great downward spiral. "The jobs that have not been here forever are the impure ones—the ones that arrived only once the world had spoiled."

Since 2017, seven months after Casciari published a version of that story in Spain's second-largest newspaper, causing a stir among the more buttoned-up members of the legal community, I've taught undergraduate journalism and public relations courses at the University of Tennessee. This side hustle teaching 20-year-olds how to write has made my work as a marketer, publicist, or whatever full-time job I'm working at the time more bearable (although the jury's out on whether a major university should be letting a guy who nearly dropped out of college to become a missionary soccer coach in Cambodia influence young minds).

During the first week of class, I ask all my students to write an essay introducing themselves and stating their career ambitions. In six years, I've yet to read any papers in which a student opts to become a clown or baker. But in 2021, I started teaching a first-year studies course and instead of making the essay their first assignment, I made it their last. All 13 students would stand before the class and give presentations about what they wanted to make of their lives once they exited the ivory tower they'd only just entered.

"I just want to retire my mom and dad," said the first to present. At least four others shared the same goal: buy their parents big houses or pay off their existing mortgages, then persuade them to retire early. "I want to open hospitals in Nigeria," said one of the students, adding that he planned to do it by 35. That way, he could retire young and spend his 40s traveling through Europe or going into business for himself. "There's time to hammer out the details," he said. Two of the students announced they would become engineers for Tesla so they'd be first in line for hovercars once they hit the mass market. Another hadn't declared a major yet but was sure he'd pack up all his possessions the day after graduation and head west to live in a van beside a beach in California. The last to go said he would move overseas to work in marketing or event planning for Liverpool Football Club in England. After a few years at the top level of European football, he'd return to the United States to work as a high school athletics director.

I wonder what I would have said at their age. In 2007, I took my first-year studies class with Susan Dinan, the director of the honors college at William Paterson University. I'd gotten accepted on a full scholarship, fulfilling my dad's request and earning the freedom to major in whatever I wanted. To his dismay, I chose Latin American and Latino studies, not a more practical subject like business or engineering. The day I visited campus, I told the admissions counselor that I was interested in the history of Argentina, the country my parents had emigrated from. He told me I was in luck because the university had just created a major that would allow me to read Jorge Luis Borges, speak Spanish, and spend a semester in South America.

Unfortunately, I didn't get the chance to study abroad, nor did I learn how to secure a decent-paying job that didn't require a master's degree. When I graduated, I wasn't ready to pay my car insurance or save up for a mortgage one day (though to be fair to my professors, they'd urged me to keep studying while I insisted I was ready for the real world). If Dinan had asked me to write an essay like the one I assign my students, I would've certainly said something along the lines of: "I want to write a book about undocumented immigrant soccer players, then become their agent and help them land professional contracts in Europe." If she'd asked me to choose something more reasonable, I would have still said writing. But I would've added traveling to beautiful places, from Easter Island to Angkor Wat, while training my children to become elite soccer players.

Even if I had said something else, I've envisioned what I'm working for ever since I fantasized about the future while sipping Snapple with Mickey and Jeremy in the kitchen. The dream always leads to a home with floor-to-ceiling mahogany bookshelves bursting with stories, histories, films, and records—the kind of place where a parent could homeschool their kids and they wouldn't turn out weird, because instead of fundamentalist lesson plans from Young Earth creationists in Pensacola they'd be absorbing the works of C. S. Lewis, Søren Kierkegaard, and Ralph Waldo Emerson.

For many years after college, I lost that dream. Or rather, I let it die. Only recently have I begun painfully resurrecting that faded, quixotic past self.

I pan the ashes of a life conformed to the hyperactive inhumanity of American capitalism for something to cherish.

In my mid-30s, I've rediscovered my imagination, trying to become what I'd wanted to be as a little boy watching the Kratt Brothers' nature shows on PBS, reading *Frankenstein* in the playroom, and frantically jotting down story ideas and song lyrics in a notepad.

Even though you can line us up and divide based on religion, politics, or favorite sports teams, every person I know is working towards identical ends. It doesn't matter who they pray to or which nation's flag they fly outside their front door. We all want healthy bodies and families. We want to be happy and hopeful. We want good schools, clean streets, and lives filled with meaning and purpose. In the better world we hope our descendants inherit, we envision vibrant neighborhoods, good intentions, and savings accounts with enough money to feast on holidays and store the rest away for vacations to the distant places our teachers had us read about in school.

So how did we stray so far from paradise? When did we stop dreaming of becoming astronauts and marine biologists and settle for careers as paper pushers and personal injury attorneys?

In "Letter to the Person Who, During the Q&A Session After the Reading, Asked for Career Advice," a beautiful, rambling poem by Matthew Olzmann, he addresses a similar point:

> *In this country, in the year I was born, some 3.1*
> *million other people were also born, each with their*

own destiny, the lines of their palms predicting an incandescent future. Were all of them supposed to be "strategy consultants" and "commodity analysts"? Waterslide companies pay people to slide down waterslides to evaluate their product. Somehow, that's an actual job. So is naming nail polish colors. Were these ever presented as options?

I'm not sure that they were. But I'm just as unsure that I'd consider leaving my stable job at the university to become a rodeo clown or a chainsaw juggler. If there's an insurance agent who'd drop their sales commissions to train as a bagpipe player in the Scottish Highlands, I've yet to meet them. The ultimate question for so many of us is the one our parents posed when we told them we wanted to major in art history. "But how much does it pay?" And it's a fair question: how many of us can pay our bills and keep our families fed by coaching high school field hockey in Alaska or recording Latin bluegrass records?

But is doing what we don't love—something that, on Monday mornings, we can't even muster the spirit to get out of bed to tolerate—really living? We work jobs we complain about over beers with our closest friends, and then we walk through our front door, drained of purpose, and lie on the couch to stream mindless TV shows so that we don't kick the dog or scream at our children.

I'm fortunate; I recognize that much. My bio says *writer* in the first sentence—or, depending on the audience, *content marketer, public relations specialist, brand storyteller,* or whatever other title I can fabricate to earn a living wage. The point is this: I get paid to sit in front of a computer and type. And even when the words are not my favorites and the name on the page is not my own, I think back to bleaker days as a bill collector and doggie daycare worker and am grateful. For generations, the callouses on the hands of my ancestors weren't formed from CrossFit. The men in my family arrange sewer pipes in the rain and tear apart car engines in stifling July heat; I reorganize my Google Drive before a Zoom meeting in a climate-controlled office suite.

Unlike the 13 students in my classroom, with their hopes and dreams still out in front of them, I can't help feeling that I've missed the boat on mine. The feeling intensifies as I get older. Despite my white-collar comforts, I've failed to meet the expectations placed on firstborns and first-generation Americans (or first-generation anything, for that matter). The writer E. Alex Jung, in a profile of director Lulu Wang after the release of *The Farewell*, said, "If children are extensions of their parents' lives, then immigrant children often contain the promise of a dream deferred."

When I was a boy, my dad took my brother and me to work plumbing jobs in the suburbs and told us in broken English that it was our responsibility to do better than he could. That if we worked hard and were smart, we'd one day live in the big houses he was paid to work in. Of my first-year studies students, at least half were the first of their families born in America. They aim to pay off the debt they owe their parents for their sacrifices and wrestle with the tension of achieving their own dreams—the ones that lead to hovercars on West Coast highways—and those they believe will make their parents happy.

Inspired by my children and my students, I recently set out looking for the cavern where I hid my boyhood dreams. When I found it, I took a sledgehammer to the walls that kept me from holding those dreams in my hands again. I'm not naive; I realize I cannot become who I imagined I would be when I was 18. Life is filled with obstacles to traverse and mountains to ascend; the only guarantee is growing older. My students will switch majors and fail classes. They'll transfer schools. Their parents may get sick, and they'll have to move back home to care for them. Instead of becoming wildlife photographers and amusement park designers, they'll work practical jobs for money, health care benefits, or retirement plans. They'll forget about opening hospitals in crisis zones and surfing at sunrise off the coast of San Diego. But they may not.

As I put the finishing touches on an early draft of this story, my two oldest, Alba and Enzo, tore apart the living room. I closed my laptop and found solace in the nature documentary *David Attenborough: A Life on Our Planet*. In the opening scene, Attenborough stands amid the ruins of Chernobyl, the site of one of history's most horrific nuclear disasters. "If only those scientists had been feeding orangutans in Borneo," I murmured to myself, "and not playing about with chemicals capable of incinerating the earth."

Over the course of an hour, Attenborough leads the viewer through the damage humanity has caused. He reveals the broken heart of our planet. But then he stops and reverses the narrative, showing what we're doing to save it: solar farms in Morocco and sustainable fishing in Palau. And by the film's end, we're back in Chernobyl. A ghost city, a place too toxic for human civilization, has become a sanctuary for bison, elk, and at least 60 rare species of animals and plants. Out of death comes life. And I can't help thinking that maybe the same is possible with our dreams—no matter how late we've started or how long we've ignored the beating inside our chests.

Fàilte gu Alba

Mu tha thu airson a bhith buan, na teid eadar an té ruadh agus a' chreag (Translation: If you want to live a long life, don't die.)

—Scottish Gaelic proverb

More than 14 years have passed since the first, and so far the last, great adventure of my life.

My childhood best friends and I had just finished our freshman year of college: Mickey at Rutgers, Jeremy at Calvin College in western Michigan, and me at William Paterson University, an hour's drive north of Bayonne. Days after returning home, we boarded a plane bound for London's Heathrow Airport on our way to Scotland, where for three weeks we explored small fishing villages and countryside hamlets, pitched our tent in the backyards of friendly strangers, and spoke late into the night about what would become of our lives once we got back home.

That year was the longest we had been apart since fourth grade. The three of us had shown up at PS 14, the magnet school for prodigies, poets, and politically connected kids from throughout Bayonne, knowing only one or two other students. Mickey and Jeremy found each other first, bonding over their shared pleasure in chucking pine cones at older kids in the park beside the school building. We became a trio a year later when Mrs. K assigned us to work on a group project we had to present weeks later in front of the entire class.

I remember the details vaguely. I think the project had something to do with creating and promoting a business or product. In our first meeting, we barely dug below the surface before uncovering what would bond us for life: we were weirdos. The proof was in the pudding. When it came time to present what we had come up with to the class, we transformed into The Boys by the Bay, whipping out fake microphones and a novelty turd and belting out a song-and-dance number about beans. The song included the line, "It sounded it like a fart, but it came out like a dart, Mr. Bean!" On the climactic note, Mickey dropped the toy turd he had been hiding to the ground, and we bowed. Our classmates looked on in a strange mix of horror and delight.

But our friendship was rooted in more than just eccentricity. We also shared an inextinguishable curiosity about the world around us. Teachers had told us there were pearls in oysters waiting to be pried open by our fingers. We only had to leave the borders of our scraggly blue-collar city to search for them. And so in 2008, at the age of 19, we booked a flight, bought two weeks' worth of train passes, and upon landing in London took a Megabus north into a country that we knew about only because we'd watched the movie *Braveheart*.

Halfway through the trip, our longing for something more landed us on the Isle of Skye. As the most responsible and meticulous member of the group, Jeremy was responsible for creating the trip's itinerary before leaving Calvin for the semester. Late one night, he had emailed to ask if we had any requests for a hike that would serve as the culmination of our foreign adventure. Mickey and I suggested "something beautiful" in a place where we could hear locals conversing in their native tongue. We didn't realize that, to Jeremy, that translated into a 22-mile hike along a ridgeline on Skye's northernmost peninsula, a death sentence for three city boys who had never hiked any longer than four miles in a day before.

We passed the Quiraing, a dazzling landscape of valleys, gorges, and mountain peaks, just two miles into our walk. From there, the trail disappeared along with any other human presence on the ridgeline. For the next eight miles, we struggled to carry our heavy backpacks up and down peaks as 40-mile-an-hour winds pelted our sunburned bodies. Past rolling green hills, breathtaking views of high-elevation lochs, and the ocean beyond were only endless flocks of sheep, which scampered away as we neared them. They must've been just as perplexed about what in the world we were doing in the middle of nowhere.

Inside our tent, eating cold lentils from Ziploc bags as the sun set over Scotland, Mickey and I were furious and exhausted. First we cursed Jeremy for stranding us on a trailless hike 3,000 miles from home. Then we cursed him for not checking the camping stove before we left to make sure it still worked. "You care more about conquering nature," Mickey said, sticking a finger in Jeremy's chest, "than enjoying it." And Jeremy responded, "Maybe overcoming it is the means to fully take pleasure in it." I didn't bother to chime in. My focus was entirely on what lay ahead: Hartaval, the second-highest peak on the Trotternish. Pissed or not, we had a decision to make.

I've been reminiscing about that three-week trip for nearly two decades, plunging myself into memories I will never recreate with people who no longer live just minutes away. Mickey, Jeremy, and I have experienced so much since 2008. But the memories of Scotland are as fresh today as they were when we made them.

For much of the trip, we relied on the generosity of strangers. In town after town, we knocked on doors and asked if we could pitch our tent in their backyards. Our first night in the country, we stayed at a hostel in Edinburgh. The next morning, we took the train to Lanark in search of the ruins of St Kentigern's Church, where William Wallace was rumored to be married. Unable to find a place to rest our heads, Mickey walked into an Oxfam store to ask if there was a hill nearby we could set up camp. He came out with a hand-drawn map from Mrs. McKinley, an older woman who lived five miles away in Ravenstruther with her eldest son, David. She said we could sleep in her garden if we managed to find the house. After we did, she invited a couple of friends over to meet the Americans who had wandered into her life. We stayed up watching the United States men's soccer team lose 2–nil to the English while eating "sausagey-burgers" and drinking Budweisers David had picked up in honor of our visit.

Stops in Glasgow, Falkirk, and Fort William followed. Two nights before crossing over to Skye we arrived in Mallaig. On our way into town, we had walked by the Fisherman's Mission. But instead of ringing the doorbell, we got a table at a nice restaurant a block away and ordered fish and chips. No friendly stranger invited us in that night, so we set up our tent on a nearby hill. The conversation ran out around 8 p.m., but the sun was still high overhead. Aggravated by the swarms of highland midges that had snuck their way inside and pricked our skin through our clothes, we wandered back to the mission, where we were invited in for dinner. Before eating, the resident fishermen sang "In Christ Alone, "Before the Throne of God Above," and other old hymns from a printout sheet. Their faces were ruddied, their beards unkempt, and they swayed in clothes that smelled of fish guts, singing:

No guilt in life, no fear in death—
This is the pow'r of Christ in me;
From life's first cry to final breath,
Jesus commands my destiny.

The next morning we took the ferry to Skye and were bused into Portree, the island's largest town. A kind couple let us keep the extra supplies from our packs—which weighed just under the airline's 50-pound limit—in their garden shed while we hiked. From their home, we traveled by bus to Flodigarry, where we listened to schoolchildren bantering in Gaelic (hearing Scotland's native language spoken aloud and James McFadden's goal against the French in Paris during Euro 2008 qualifiers were secondary motivations for our trip). We used the facilities at the hostel to cook the lentils we later ate cold after Jeremy's camping stove failed. And we chatted late into the night about Scottish politics, romance, and American culture with Bryan, the graying hostel worker who drove us to the trailhead the following day.

I can't speak for my friends, but I've always felt like a package delivered to the wrong address. I felt that way at college in North Jersey. I haven't shaken the feeling decades later in Knoxville. So before the fall semester of 2008, I told other students at William Paterson that my dad had been a footballer in Argentina who moved to Britain to play for Hearts, and that we relocated to the States after he retired because it was better than the alternative of being economically unstable in their homeland. I put on my best Edinburgh English accent to recount the story each time. I doubt now that any of my classmates believed it. But keeping up the fiction distracted me from the melancholy of settling back into my routine. Every day, I longed to go back. At night when I shut my eyelids, I was transported to Skye. I'd wake up in a sweaty daze and look for the next flight from JFK, despite knowing that I'd never board it.

Looking back in time appeals to nostalgics because it allows us to see the various starting points from which we could have taken roads to other places. We imagine alternate routes or stopovers along the way. But there's a tragic element to setting our sights on the past. Mickey and Jeremy knew me better than anyone. When Ben Rector released the song "Old Friends" in 2018, they were the first people I thought of. Through our time at PS 14 and in high school, we lived within a dozen blocks of each other. We would walk or bike to each other's houses at least once a week. We played music and soccer together and spent Friday nights in Mickey's attic ordering pizza and drinking Snapple as we fantasized about girls and faraway lands. We planned our entire lives out, never imagining the others wouldn't be along for the ride. Then, one by one, we left. And we've not returned for longer than to see our parents.

After college, Mickey moved to Miami, then Haiti, and now the Dominican Republic. Jeremy returned from Michigan and has lived within a 45-minute drive of Bayonne since. I left for Knoxville, thinking my time in the South would be a two-year diversion at best. I fantasized about future moves to Argentina, Cambodia, DC, Atlanta, and Denver that never materialized. Odds are my life will end here, a city where my children were born and my wife's roots are deeper in the soil than my family's in this country.

When we're young, there's a voice inside our heads whispering that things won't always be the same. Friends will come and go. We'll grow up and move away from each other. The voice tells us that we should vacuum-seal the moments we're together and store them somewhere safe. Because the sand will only deepen at the bottom of the hourglass. And by our 30s, we'll live in different zip codes, have families of our own, new hobbies, and careers we could have never imagined in the days when we sipped iced tea in our parents' kitchens and bought plane tickets to a foreign land because we liked a Mel Gibson movie from the '90s.

The morning after camping on Skye, we woke up in no mood to tackle Hartaval. Unrelenting winds coming through the valley had blasted our tent throughout the night. Our heads were pounding and our bodies sore enough that getting through the remaining dozen miles to the Old Man of Storr, the trail's natural stopping point, without killing each other seemed unlikely. So we scrambled down a dried-up waterfall near our campsite and walked through miles of spongy flat land until we could almost see the road back to Portree.

The only barrier keeping us from hitchhiking back to warm food and beds was a forest thick with pine trees. Somewhere in those pines, the digital camera Mickey had brought to document the trip fell out of the unzipped pocket of his Sweden track jacket. In that camera were hundreds of irreplaceable photos—of Mrs. McKinley, Old Edinburgh, New Lanark, the monsterless lochs of Inverness, and Jeremy's Polish friends who met us in Glasgow and drove us in their rented van through the green Highlands, where we occasionally stopped to listen to a lone bagpiper playing "Scotland the Brave." After realizing it, Mickey's body gave out, and he cried out hopelessly into the floor of loose pine needles.

Eventually, he settled his nerves and we made it to the road, where I kissed the gravel, and a van driver from Staffin drove us to a hostel. But we grieved the loss, knowing we could never put those photos into albums that we'd flip through with our grandchildren—that I could never say to my daughter, "Here we are in the land I named you after."

We photograph so much nowadays. If we had traveled to Scotland in 2023, we would've each had a smartphone in our pockets ready to capture images we could post to social media for loved ones and strangers to like and comment on. But in 2008, smartphones weren't ubiquitous yet, and the only place you could regularly access WiFi was at the library—where we went to send emails to our parents and girlfriends to let them know we were OK. The images that would've populated our Facebook feeds were lost among the trees.

Fortunately, I've held on to some. They hang safely in frames on display in the cavernous hallways of my mind palace, where I venture on gloomy days to remember who we were then. Among the images, I see Mickey's smile from when his hair was long and tied back in a ponytail and he wore black hoodies over soccer jerseys and jeans ripped at the hem. I see Jeremy in his favorite heather gray T-shirt as we drove on his 18th birthday to watch *300* at Frank Theatres, which today sits abandoned, a relic of our youth. Later that day, we gathered to eat cake and share stories of our friendship with those outside our inner circle. Mickey and I had filmed a video for the occasion, a throwback to Mrs. K's class. In it, we wore a pile of plastic shopping bags on our heads to imitate Jeremy's golden afro from that time. There was no song-and-dance number. But we did mimic him memorizing a phone book, creating a solar system, and getting lost in the kind of pencil-wielding, air-drumming euphoria that drew the ire of our teachers.

Most of the time when I picture us, though, we're back on Skye, huddled inside our tent. The resentment from the brutal hike is gone, and we laugh as we try to imagine what the future will look like once we return home. As our eyelids grow heavy with sleep, we lay our heads down for the night. The trail is not yet finished, the journey not quite over. And once we board the plane back to America, nothing will ever be the same.

In Memoriam to My Emo Years

The show was on April 30, 2010. I know that because, not wanting to go alone, I had posted about it on Facebook. It had been years since I'd seen The Early November, but I'd kept up with Ace Enders, the band's frontman. So when he announced he was playing a solo show that night at Ramapo College, I knew I couldn't miss it.

Adam, my former bandmate, joined me for the drive from Bayonne to the unremarkable university building where Enders—a heavyweight figure of the emo music scene that had pervaded New Jersey's suburbs throughout the 2000s—was set to open for River City Extension. I was a junior at William Paterson University. My hair was no longer dyed black and swept over the left side of my face. My T-shirts and jeans were no longer skintight. But for three years in high school, I had proudly identified as a scenester—the in-group term for emo kids. Even though my musical tastes had expanded by the time I left for college, The Early November was one of the few bands I never felt ashamed to love.

Mickey and I discovered the band on a DVD released by Drive-Thru Records, the preeminent emo label of our teenage years. It featured a live version of "Every Night's Another Story" recorded at Skate and Surf, which was like Bonnaroo for New Jersey emo kids in the age before smartphones. During most of the summer of 2003, we watched that DVD, which included music videos, live performances, and behind-the-scenes footage of bands like Senses Fail, Newfound Glory, and The Starting Line, before practicing with our own band, Catullus. Mickey and I named the band after a Roman poet we learned about in English class; his tragic lines, inspired by his unrequited love for a married aristocratic woman, were sufficiently emo, and the name was superior to the alternatives, Candlehat Suicide and The Agony of Defeat. Mickey would get behind his drum kit, I'd strap on my bass, and Adam—who was two years younger than us and 100 times as talented—grabbed his guitar. (Mickey had recruited Adam while playing hacky sack during recess, and he tried out as our lead guitarist with the solo from "Hell Song" by Sum 41.) We turned up our amps and played songs about teenage heartbreak until dark when the neighbors doubled down on noise complaints to the police.

Somehow in that age before social media, Mickey had found out that The Early November and all the other Drive-Thru bands we loved were playing on October 17, 2003, at Club Krome, a rundown venue in either Sayreville or South Amboy (depending on what you Google). Despite being 14, we convinced our parents to drop us off an hour away and pick us up after 10 p.m. For four hours, we lifted our hands to the ceiling, screamed our throats raw, and surfed on the fingertips of strangers. In the parking lot after a break between bands, Buddy Nielsen, the frontman of Senses Fail, signed our arms with a black marker. We refused to shower that night so we could proudly show off his signature, which had come to resemble a black blob by morning, to the five other kids at Bayonne High School who knew what emo music was.

I don't know how we come to the genres of music we love. My first favorite band was the Spice Girls. In third grade, I forced my parents to take me to see *Spice World* at the rundown movie theater at Hudson Mall in Jersey City. (My dad fell asleep within 10 minutes.) In fourth and fifth grade, my favorite band was the Backstreet Boys. In sixth grade, a year after performing "As Long as You Love Me" a cappella during music class, I asked my dad to buy me Blink-182's *Enema of the State* at K-Mart.

Mark Hoppus, Tom DeLonge, and Travis Barker held the top spot until eighth grade when I bought a ball-chain necklace and a System of a Down T-shirt and told everyone my favorite band was Cold. Nü metal was a form-fitting genre for a chubby kid on the wrong side of the popular crowd. Then Mickey and I found emo, and it became the defining genre of our youth. For me, it's hard to argue that it still isn't. Ben Howard, Bon Iver, Sufjan Stevens—are they not the emo music of dads approaching middle age?

During the first half of my high school life, in the time before iPods and universal streaming, I owned a yellow Walkman CD player. Back and forth from school, I'd have The Early November's 2003 album *The Room's Too Cold* on without interruption. I bought it at Sound City on Broadway, where my friends and I loitered for hours until our musical appetite became so insatiable that we turned to Ares, Kazaa, and Limewire to get our fix for free.

Each fall, when the average high drops below 70 and the trees shed their leaves, I turn on a Spotify playlist I've been curating since December 15, 2014. As of August 2023, it contains nearly 11 hours of emo songs released between 2002 and 2006. When it plays in the car, I remember the many Saturday nights spent at VFW halls and music venues around New Jersey with my friends, my dyed hair cascading over my left eye in a waterfall of sadness. If a genie had been around then to grant me a wish, I would have asked for Catullus to get signed to a record label big enough to pay for us to tour the country. In that imaginary world, I'd sing my dreadful lyrics over a crowd of other dudes in desperate need of girlfriends. After the show, a cute girl with snakebite piercings would ask to make out with me.

In 2017, the writer Mabel Rosenheck wrote for *Longreads* about the nostalgia she feels for her own days as an emo kid in New Jersey. In her essay, she points out the misogyny, lack of self-awareness, and immaturity of the scene we both shared. Her words make me wince each time I listen closely to the lyrics sung by the guys in Hawthorne Heights and Coheed and Cambria. Rosenheck writes:

> *Though I clearly indulge in it, nostalgia is a problematic mode of understanding the past. It is too often . . . about a time and place that is romanticized, a time and place that never really existed quite as we want to remember it. My memories seem so real, so accurately recalled, but I know better than to trust them. I know that memories lie, and yet I believe mine. . . . Mine are memories that want to find a place in the present . . . but they are memories which I fear are simply naive artifacts of the past. They are artifacts I'm not sure I should retrieve. They are artifacts I'm not sure how to retrieve anyway.*

And yet I can tell you, without question, that some of the nights I cherish most from my adolescence are the ones spent in Mickey's attic after Catullus practice, blasting Silverstein from our iPods, eating 28-inch pizzas and Double Stuf Oreos, and talking about venues for our first national tour once we got signed to Drive-Thru, Victory, or Equal Vision Records.

That tour never materialized because, in the end, it turned out Catullus wasn't very good. Our lyrics were generic, and aside from Adam, whose band Gatherers did eventually sign to Equal Vision, the musicianship was unremarkable. Mickey and I would not become rock stars. And even though we never spoke about it, in our more lucid moments I'm sure we knew that the most important thing in the world was not hooking up with girls. Even if it had been, would lamenting about our celibacy over a beat and a breakdown really have made us more attractive to them?

Listening to Ace Enders today, I realize he wasn't the lyrical genius I made him out to be. He was an angsty kid from suburban South Jersey, just a few years older than me, experimenting with poetic ways of talking about relationships with girls and his parents. His songs were catchy, though the lyrics made little sense. Take the chorus to "Ever So Sweet," the first and most famous song from *The Room's Too Cold*:

> *Ever so sweet, you baked it in cakes for me*
> *What you left behind, it hurts my teeth*
> *Bring in the past, with the postcards you sent for me*
> *Every line, it brings me right back down.*

But to Ace's credit, even as the genre slumped out of the mainstream and became a memento for those of us who had cut our hair and traded our band tees for polo shirts and flannels, he never stopped writing and recording new songs. When Adam and I went to his Ramapo College show, The Early November had been officially broken up for four years. So Ace was releasing music under two names: Ace Enders and a Million Different People, and I Can Make a Mess Like Nobody's Business. He was prolific and maturing. Eventually the band got back together and released five more albums. In total, Ace Enders has released 15 full-length albums, seven EPs, and dozens of singles across all his acts and pseudonyms. At 41, he's as prolific as Paul Simon, Dolly Parton, and Elvis Costello.

I've realized—largely thanks to Spotify—that the artists we once loved don't disappear the second we tune out. Today I pinpoint former emo kids in coffee shops by the gaping holes in their ears from where plugs once were. One time at Remedy Coffee, I noticed an Underoath sticker on the water bottle of a balding dude with thick-rimmed glasses and colorful tattoo sleeves. We struck up a nostalgic conversation, and I said, "I really liked Underoath too, before their new stuff got weird." And by their new stuff, I meant any album recorded after 2006. When I get a notification on Spotify about new releases from bands like Taking Back Sunday and Armor for Sleep, I have to pause and make sure I'm reading it right. Who could their music possibly be for now? Surely not this generation of scenesters. Or are Gen Z kids discovering the emo music of yesteryear the way I found Bruce Springsteen and John Prine decades after their first wave of ardent followers?

At Ramapo College, Ace Enders strummed an electric guitar he hooked up to an effects pedal that made it sound like he was playing in outer space. He asked if anyone had song requests, and I did: "Just Enough"—a song that was never released but appeared in acoustic form on the Drive-Thru Records DVD Mickey and I watched obsessively that summer of 2003. I did it to let Ace know he had a real fan there, a kid who had walked eight blocks to school humming the words that he had written in his basement two hours away. Ace was as surprised as I had hoped he would be. "I don't remember how to play that one," he said. "But if you do, why don't you come up here and play it with me?" I couldn't accept the invitation because I didn't know how to play it either.

The show ended, and I waited patiently behind other fans to talk with Ace before the next band played. After the demise of Catullus, I quit writing songs about girls and started writing blog posts about philosophy, colonialism, and the tension between traditional masculinity and wanting to cry for reasons other than that my favorite sports team lost. Assuming that Ace also had a thing for Ernest Hemingway or Chuck Palahniuk, I asked who his favorite writer was. "Bryan Adams," he said in a soft voice. "No, I mean writer of books," I explained. "Oh, I don't read much," Ace said. "I'm sort of dyslexic." And that was that. Adam and I got in the car and drove back to Bayonne, listening to Dance Gavin Dance and The Dangerous Summer—bands that formed the second wave of emo music in my life. This less demanding time didn't require girls' jeans, black eyeliner, or telling people that mainstream bands like Good Charlotte and Simple Plan were posers.

From what I can uncover online, Ace Enders and The Early November have yet to play a show in Knoxville. I occasionally check to see if he's planning a tour with a stop in Nashville or Atlanta so I can be there in the front row. Today the band members are all in their 40s, with wives and children. Their songs are about different kinds of heartbreak. But when I ask Alexa to play *Twenty*, *Lilac,* or any other album from the past 20 years, I sometimes catch sight of myself in the bedroom mirror. Returning my gaze is a much younger version of me in ball-crushing jeans and a shirt he stole from Hot Topic. *He's going to miss this,* I think, as the sound of one of my children wailing from across the hallway snaps me back to reality.

The Writing on the Bathroom Wall

The truth will set you free. But not until it is finished with you.

—David Foster Wallace, *Infinite Jest*

It was a cold Friday night in January when I suddenly got a message from the past, written on the wall of a bathroom stall inside Barley's.

Haley and I had just moved our family into the new house in Halls, and I hadn't really felt like going out when David (aka *El Boliviano*) invited the dads in our WhatsApp group to celebrate his birthday in the Old City. The week leading up to it had been long. Changes at work had me anxious about the future. The kids, tiny disease magnets that they are, were fighting off strep throat and ear infections. A few days earlier, on Tuesday, Mickey had touched down for 36 hours just as I was supposed to be finishing work projects I had dragged out since before Christmas.

But because I'm a people pleaser at my core, I told my friends I'd meet them once the kids were asleep and my wife turned on *Jeopardy*. Even though I assumed it'd be a small gathering like it usually is for the birthday parties of the other Tribesman, *El Boliviano* is a human extension cord. He had invited all his neighbors, who can best be described as the kinds of people who live in remodeled Craftsman houses and drink IPAs. Since I only recently started collecting vinyl records and have functioning taste buds, I had little to contribute to the conversation. But there was a jam band with a horn section playing; the lead singer wore a top hat and feather boa, which I thought was fun. So I hung around until I'd filled my bladder with enough Miller High Life that I needed a bathroom break.

If you've been inside Barley's, you know there are two men's rooms: one upstairs full of band stickers and graffiti and one downstairs that is nice. I chose the first because I like to read the chains of messages people carve into the walls. Between the *MP <3 JK 2018*s and *Bama Sucks*, you get the occasional trivia question or joke. (What do you call a dog that lives in your toilet? A poo-dle.) These are typically followed by insults about the writer's sexual orientation or Nick Saban's grandmother. I followed one chain of messages down until I saw a phrase that looked like it had been carved into the stall with a pocketknife and then written over with black ink:

Yo Tipsy, what's good? :)

I chuckled at first. Tipsy is what Mickey had called me in high school. It stuck for a while, and I hated it. But then I saw a black line from the message that skirted down past some other writings before arriving at its final destination: a phone number—a 201 number. The hair on my arms stood up. In a decade, I've met only a handful of Knoxvillians who've even heard of Hudson County, the New Jersey county to which that area code—my area code—is assigned. Scribbled underneath the number, in parentheses:

Still looking for me? ;)

It was signed *Viktor Jankula.*

Here's where some further explanation is required. Viktor Jankula was an acquaintance from elementary school. Calling him a friend is a stretch, considering how little I remember about him. What I do remember is that he was half Peruvian and half Czech. We were both accepted into PS 14, the magnet school we attended from fourth to eighth grade, for art. And because our moms spoke Spanish and Hispanic kids were vastly outnumbered at the school, we hung out from time to time. His parents' apartment had a room with dead butterflies in glass cases. The way they hung frozen on the wall fascinated me.

Viktor was a troublemaker, rougher around the edges than I was. My most vivid memory of our friendship is from the winter of sixth grade when he came on vacation with my family to the Pocono Mountains. I've got pictures of us inside an igloo we built. He invited me skiing with his dad a few times that year, but I declined because I was afraid of hurdling down the mountain to my death. After we finished eighth grade, he went off to a private school in Jersey City, and I never heard from him again—though, for some reason I can't fully explain, I've searched Facebook for evidence of what happened to him ever since.

Since Mickey moved to the Dominican Republic and I made a more permanent life in Knoxville, whenever we get together we reminisce about people like Viktor Jankula—former classmates and friends we haven't seen in two decades. On the list beside his name are Britney Micele, Don Sim, Megan Dwyer, James Wekwert, Amy Buccafusco: the ones who haven't shown up to class reunions or who we don't run into at bars or walking their dogs at the park when we're back home visiting our parents. *Where had they gone?*

I think it's second nature for those of us who grew up before smartphones, when relationships were rooted in real experiences we couldn't catalog for people to scroll past on social media, to create mental lists of childhood acquaintances and wonder about their lives since we'd last seen them. Our memories hang frozen like butterflies in glass cases. They surface only once we've put down our phones and let our minds drift back in time. First Myspace and later Facebook provided us with a means to find the people we had lost. We no longer had to guess what became of old friends and neighbors; we looked them up by name and city. Some we found and reconnected with. Others created profiles they hadn't updated in years; to this day, the only posts on their feeds are birthday messages from relatives. The rest either never bought into social media or deleted their accounts before we began searching for them. They've floated like ghosts in the periphery of our minds, where we can't update their voices or faces.

I zipped up and texted the phone number before flushing. The bubble on my iPhone was green. *Maybe it's a landline,* I thought. I walked out of the bathroom and straight to the parking lot, where I sat in my Honda Civic, staring at my phone, not sure what to do next.

I texted the phone number again and waited for a response while deciding whether to drive home or send Mickey a WhatsApp message. I wondered if somehow he had written the message those few days he was in town. The only other person who'd visited me and also known Viktor—Jeremy, my other best friend—had been in for just one night the summer before. *Impossible,* I thought.

Just then, my phone rang. *Scam likely,* it said on the screen. The location was Bayonne, New Jersey. I let it go to voicemail. The caller didn't leave a message. But they called again and again—four times before finally leaving a short message.

"Oh, come on, Carnivore," a man's voice said, muddled, as if he were chewing on potato chips. "Pick up the phone."

I looked up from my screen: a giant in black sunglasses stood in the yellow beam of the headlights.

"Holy crap!" I blurted out with the windows closed.

Patrick Finerty motioned to the passenger seat. "You think you're the only person who looks for Viktor on Facebook?" he asked as he squeezed all six feet, 300-something pounds of his body into my Civic.

I hadn't seen Finerty since eighth grade, though I'd heard rumors about him. My brother went camping with friends near the Delaware Water Gap once and told me Finerty had shown up, wandering in the background like he was looking for something that wasn't there. "He didn't look good," he told me on the phone. But the guy I was looking at years later still resembled the kid I'd sat next to in fifth grade and traded Pokémon cards with. His hairline was further back on his forehead, his voice more gravelly, but this was undoubtedly him.

"We look you up, too," he said, reclining to the point that he hit the base of Alba's car seat. "We know what you've been up to."

"That's ominous," I said. I could feel the hair on my arms sticking up again.

Finerty pointed at my phone. "Unlock it," he said, motioning for me to hand it over. He went to my recent calls list, tapped the first number, and put the call on speaker. He rested the phone face up on his enormous left thigh.

The man from the voicemail answered. "Tipsy!" Viktor shouted, hanging on the last syllable.

"We're all here. The ones you've been searching for." Other voices murmured in the background. "We've been watching you, too. Waiting for the right time to surface." Viktor's voice sounded like a cross between Anton Chigurgh and Hannibal Lecter. "When we saw Mickey board that plane, we decided it was time to write you."

He referred to his group as The Undiscoverables. Occasionally, he explained, they created a LinkedIn profile. But they were careful not to upload a profile picture or complete their work histories. They were on Twitter but never tweeted. They placed clues in far corners of the internet, pages deep into Google searches. I'd looked there before, finding a blurry image and clicking just to end up with a broken link—a trail of jellybeans to a cliff's edge.

"That was all part of the plan," Viktor said. "But even after you stepped back, your spirit didn't break. You kept wandering over to the edge to see if you'd catch sight of us."

I wanted to say something. Finerty, sensing it, put his left forearm in front of my chest. *Don't speak, just listen*, he mouthed.

Viktor hadn't called to answer questions. All the ones I'd been asking myself, trying to find the answers to for 20 years with Mickey and Jeremy—*Had he fit in at St. Peter's Prep with the other private school kids? Did his parents leave Bayonne? Did he finish college? Get married? Have kids?*—were to remain a mystery.

"Can you at least get on FaceTime or Zoom?" I asked. Finerty glared into my soul. I wanted to see if time had aged Viktor as it had me—if his hair was still black and spiky or thinned and receded like mine, if there were glimmers of the person I once knew.

"No, Tipsy," Viktor said, sounding agitated. "That's why we send Pat. That's the whole point—you don't *need* to see us. Why look for us if we've made it clear we don't want to be found? The people you knew are gone."

I'd lost my calm by that point. "How do you even know I'm looking for you, Viktor?" I asked, shouting into the phone. My passenger's gaze met mine. *We can't tell you that,* Finerty said, sternly, again without words.

But Viktor didn't need to explain. A week doesn't pass without an email from Experian or Comcast that my information has been leaked. Google follows with a notification that my passwords have been compromised again. Hackers hover in the dark of a Belarusian basement with my credit card information scrolling past pictures I deleted from Facebook in 2012. Nothing is as hidden as it was back when Viktor Jankula and I rummaged through his dad's drawers looking at the butterflies he hadn't yet hung, marveling at their colors and talking about God knows what—because, really, only God could have; neither of us had home internet yet.

Viktor reiterated his point. "Just because you choose to live your life in public doesn't mean we do," he said. The Undiscoverables protect every detail, leaving only enough crumbs out in the daylight to trick the mice who pursue them. They are the ones whose birth records and Social Security numbers Mark Zuckerberg doesn't yet have access to.

"What does it matter to you anyway, Tipsy?" he asked. "What is knowing? Why should you know everything?" And with that, he ended the call.

I looked at Finerty: a giant squeezed into a clown car. A headache was coming on. I rubbed the top of my forehead, unsure if it was real or an elaborate ruse—like the time in fifth grade Nicole Rossi convinced me the Backstreet Boys were at her house for the Super Bowl. Looking through the front windshield, I saw a hipster from *El Boliviano's* party waiting for his Uber. I pictured the others inside, smiling and laughing as they drank expensive beer and listened to the jam band, unaware of everything taking place just 30 feet away. I wondered if my friend had thought of those missing from the room besides me: the people who had been present for the previous 42 birthdays who were now long gone.

Finerty interrupted my train of thought. "So do you want to get Waffle House?" he asked. "There aren't any in New Jersey, and I have to start back tonight."

At least I learned that much: they were all still home somewhere, like bats in the shadows or turkeys in June. Where doesn't matter, because I'll never see them again unless they choose to let me.

"Your music or mine?" I asked Finerty. He chuckled, as if I should've known the answer before asking. I put on a random Spotify playlist and started toward I-40. He lifted his left hand and wagged his meaty finger in front of my face. "Not out west. Go to the one up north on Maynardville Pike. It's closer to your house. And you've had a long week."

Bugging Out

Although my mom keeps the trophies I won as a kid displayed on a shelf in my old bedroom, alongside cut-out clips from newspapers I wrote for when I thought I'd be a journalist, my accomplishments through the first 30 years of my life are nothing to write home about. They range from the unremarkable—youth soccer championships, Boy Scout merit badges, regional writing awards—to the absurd.

I take tremendous pride in my Scottish accent. My ability to pinpoint most non-Pacific Island countries on a map and match them to the correct flag is impressive to at least two other nerds I grew up with. And our senior year of high school, Mrs. Merkowski really did call me—not Jeremy, my best friend and our eventual valedictorian—the most erudite of writers in front of our entire English class. But for many years, the top spot on my podium of achievements was reserved solely for a streak that stretched back to March 22, 2004, a date I clung to like a sailor to the mast of a sinking ship.

For that was the last time I had vomited. And while not throwing up is a feat for which there is no trophy, like smacking a golf ball farthest at the driving range or emerging victorious in a belching contest, the adulation of my male brethren was reward enough.

But in the words of Robert Frost, nothing gold can stay, and my streak broke early on the morning of January 1, 2016, at Jairo's house in Fountain City. A group of about a dozen friends had gathered there to celebrate New Year's. Jairo and his wife, who'd met on a study abroad in France, had laid out an array of European cheeses, which we downed with many bottles of red wine. We toasted the evening with dancing and cheap champagne. At 5 a.m., I emerged from underneath the *Frozen* blanket his wife had covered me in after I passed out on their sunroom couch and raced to the bathroom.

I placed an asterisk on the streak that afternoon while lying on my couch eating toast and sipping yellow Gatorade. I could still say I had not thrown up *due to non-alcohol-related illness* for 14 years. The exemption remained valid through a second incident the following year—the culprit, this time, greasy fried chicken and Barcelo rum with Mickey in Santo Domingo. And it held firm through a third challenge in 2018 on the morning after my bachelor party, when I showed up groggy at my friend Patrick's house on Deadrick Ave. an hour before the start of the World Cup final and was pointed directly to the toilet.

At bonfires and over beers with friends, I boasted about my impenetrable immune system. My hubris was grounded in control—the belief that if I vomited, it was *only* because I had willingly bypassed the security system and opened the door to the enemy myself. That false sense of control lasted until February 2022.

Only a week before, Haley had told me some of her close friends had been eviscerated by the stomach bug. I listened as one does to the story of a break-in across town, responding "Oh gosh, that's terrible," while not registering the threat to my own household.

Days later, I was writhing in agony on the bathroom floor, pleading for God's healing touch over my intestines. I texted Haley the final wishes for my funeral. I gave her access to Google folders with the hundreds of letters and poems I'd written for her and the children and told her to find solace in them while lying in bed a widow. In my delirium, I wondered how we could mobilize billions of dollars to fight the coronavirus and not yet have a cure to overcome the stomach bug. *Does the government not employ the parents of small children?*

With the trauma of that February still at the forefront of my memory, last winter arrived, and I was fully aware of my vulnerability. From the first rainy December afternoon when the temperature didn't rise above 40, I paced the house in fear and trepidation because I was sure of only two things: that the bandit would show, and that once he was through the door, I'd be helpless to stop him.

The virus arrived the second week of January.

By then, my family had already overcome the flu and strep throat. I held firm longest, keeping a clean bill of health as illness downed Haley and the children. Then Leviathan descended, ravaging my insides and pushing all it could through my body's two major exit points, sometimes simultaneously.

While lying on the bathroom floor, I vowed to never again drink brown liquor or eat raw seafood and greasy fried chicken. I asked God to put a hedge of protection around me and promised that, if He did, I'd be a good boy forever. As I waited for his response, I reflected on the past and remembered that after Santo Domingo and the final at Patrick's, once the haze of illness had lifted, it had taken just hours for me to wash down cheeseburgers with fernet and Coca-Cola. I was an unreliable petitioner. So to show God I was serious, I committed to starting a new streak as soon as my illness succumbed. I would build up a foundation of good health like sandbags to protect against calamity. I'd eat peanut butter toast instead of sausage biscuits, and turkey bacon instead of pork. I'd finish my last bottle of Coke, then purchase a half-gallon water jug I'd carry with me like a high-school wrestler.

But who was I kidding? Even as I said the words to myself, I knew I'd never follow through. I am an amnesiac with a depressing lack of self-control. Hopefulness is but a veneer.

Every Sunday morning after the congregation sings the Doxology and the pastor dismisses us, I leave through the church doors feeling so light. My burdens lifted from my shoulders, I go out into the world determined to become a more loving husband, a more patient father, and a better friend. Rather than focusing on growing my newsletter subscribers or increasing my salary, I turn my attention to growing in kindness and generosity. In my journal, I write that, from that day forward, I will complain less and be grateful more. I will give and not take, pray and not scroll.

Hours later, the children wake screaming from their afternoon naps and the top layer of my resolve splinters. By Monday morning, the veneer has shattered completely. My hopefulness is replaced by task lists, emails, and anxiety about the future. I know there is no secret formula for feeling grateful instead of stressed out, just as there is no vaccine for the stomach bug. But I wish there were some midway point between pride and desolation—a powder, perhaps, that I could mix into my oatmeal every morning. Then I could take less pleasure in pointless streaks and feats. I wouldn't have to worry about everything. I'd accept that sometimes, despite prayers and probiotics, there isn't much you can do to prevent illness. Bad days will follow good ones. And no matter how much I love the leaves in autumn, winter will come—but eventually it will make way for spring.

My most recent bout with the stomach bug culminated in a pounding headache I couldn't shake. I figured out why pretty quickly. Most days, I drink two cups of coffee before 10 a.m. and another in the afternoon. But while I was sick, I avoided caffeine, knowing it'd send me right back to the toilet before my insides had fully healed. The withdrawal wasn't as bad as hurling but was painful nonetheless. And in the midst of that pain, I came up with a fresh list of self-improvement efforts. I pledged to no longer be dependent on anything. I'd wean myself off caffeine, fatty foods, carbs, and alcoholic beverages. The promise echoed the one I make each time I see myself shirtless in the mirror or fail to hit a writing deadline because I've gotten distracted watching soccer compilations on YouTube. "Time to get serious about discipline," I say, picturing a future me with six-pack abs typing away at the final pages of a book before joining Haley in an infinity pool overlooking the Pacific Ocean.

But the deeper issue is not that I daydream about tomorrow. It's that I'm a hypocrite today. I am the Apostle Paul, who writes in his Epistle to the Romans, "I don't really understand myself, for I want to do what is right, but I don't do it. Instead, I do what I hate." And as I look to friends who keep their promises and eschew vices like salt and tobacco, I justify my dependencies to avoid going through the brutal process of self-discipline. I must drink caffeine because I'm tired. I don't have the time to work out any harder. I won't eat any healthier because it takes too long to prepare a home-cooked meal when I'm trying to keep so many other plates spinning (and meat-lovers pizzas are one of life's greatest pleasures). Yet even as I play mind games with myself, I keep my attention centered on other hypocrites. Instead of a best-selling writer floating in an infinity pool, I see staring back at me in the mirror an obese preacher railing against the soullessness of

America while appealing to the congregation for a private jet so he can spread the word in Africa.

I once saw a banner in a grade-school classroom that read, "Awareness is key." Considering I still haven't mastered it as a dad in my 30s, I think it's wise to begin teaching our children to be mindful of their actions, the people around them, and what they put into their bodies as early as possible. After experiencing the joy of gummy worms and chocolate chip cookies, if my daughter knows they're in the house, she will pick at dinner, telling us she's not feeling hungry. Then minutes later, she's at the kitchen counter asking for a snack. "I've got celery if your belly's hungry," Haley tells her from the table, refusing to budge to a three-year-old's whims. Alba learns quickly and asks for her dinner plate back.

Ultimately, I must accept that only some nights will end with chocolate chips (and almost none with celery). There will be days when my body hurts and everything seems to go wrong, and other days when I'm relieved to find I haven't pulled a muscle in my sleep, my car drives just fine, and there's enough money left over in the checking account to rent an Airbnb in Hilton Head before the third baby's born. In life, I will succeed and screw up. I will string together streaks and I will crumble, hunched over a toilet bowl, texting Haley not to come inside the bathroom because I've soiled myself.

That last admission comes from a text message I sent her at the pinnacle of my lost battle against the stomach bug. Later, when she told me how she'd screenshotted it and sent it to her friends, I laughed. Because all things will pass in time, even text messages. I cannot get so wrapped up in today's troubles that I lose hope for tomorrow, just as I cannot hope so vehemently for tomorrow that I forget it isn't guaranteed. So I will make every effort today, even when my stomach is cramping and I'm cradled in the fetal position on the bathroom floor, to lift my head, put my fingers to the toilet handle, and flush.

Champions of the World

The most incredible thing about miracles is that they happen.

—GK Chesterton

The pits of my eyes were dry by the time Kylian Mbappé stepped up to take the first kick of the penalty shootout for France. It was 12:49 p.m. The rivers I had cried for 120 minutes had dried like creek beds on my cheeks, and my body shook uncontrollably as if I were freezing to death inside an Alaskan school bus. Except I was in the basement, alone, my phone set to Do Not Disturb. The only light emanated from a small lamp in the corner furthest from the television. I was watching the World Cup final—the most important event in the world—inside a cave.

"If you start feeling your arm tingle, call 911," Haley texted when I told her that I thought I was going to collapse. She had grown used to this. Since September, she had seen me cry at least 16,327 times. In the middle of the day, she would walk into the kitchen, where I'd be weeping in the corner. Instinctively, she would hug me from behind, seeping her warmth and hopefulness into my skin. But it wouldn't last long. Hours later, I'd wake up gasping for air, my body covered in sweat. "Darling, the children are asleep. Your parents are alive. We'll be in the new house before Christmas. Everything is OK," she'd reassure me, caressing my cheek. And I'd moan, "It's not that. It's Messi. I'm never going to see him play for Argentina again."

The morning of the World Cup final, Haley left the house early with the children. After 29 days of watching me suffer through Argentina's unexpected loss to Saudi Arabia, excruciating wins against Mexico and Australia, and an agonizing penalty kick shootout against the Netherlands, she understood the stakes and decided it would be better for them to watch at her mom's house. For nearly a month, I had skipped the gym, canceled plans with people I care about, left home early and worked late, had little fun, and endured inextinguishable anguish for 90 minutes at a time. After Argentina's opening loss, which Haley and I watched together on the couch as the children slept, we made a pact. For the do-or-die matchup against Mexico, I would need to be alone. She'd leave the house for 90 minutes. And if it proved a winning formula, we would not take the risk of breaking the practice until after the final whistle on December 18. I could not be the reason for Argentina's elimination.

It may not make sense to you unless you're Argentinian, have watched soccer games in Latin America, or bear the curse of having a superstitious sports fanatic in your life. Every Argentinian understands that when your team wins, you must watch the next game in exactly the same way. You must wear exactly the same thing, sit or stand in exactly the same spot, drink exactly the same drink, scratch exactly the same spot on your inner left thigh at the 53-minute mark—or risk unleashing God's fury. This is *cábala*, a tradition that stretches back to the first time a person on Argentine soil kicked a soccer ball that would've struck the post if not for a lucky pair of unwashed underwear.

The week of the semifinal against Croatia, Haley and I had taken a tremendous risk: we traveled with the children to New Jersey to visit my parents and grandparents. I had planned to watch the game alone in my parents' apartment, wearing my Argentina jersey and scarf, a flag draped over my legs—just as I had watched the wins against Mexico, Poland, Australia, and the Netherlands. But then I thought of Nono watching alone downstairs. Before moving away in 2011, I had spent a decade watching CONMEBOL qualifiers, World Cups, Champions Leagues and La Liga, Serie A, and Premier League matches with Nono at his kitchen table. On Saturdays, we would drink fernet and sweet vermouth, eat plates of mortadella, capicola, and other cold cuts we'd picked up from the Egyptian-owned Italian deli four blocks away, and watch matches from 7:30 a.m. till 6 p.m. like it was our full-time job. My friends didn't understand it. My girlfriends didn't understand it. But this was our tradition.

A month or two before every World Cup since 2010, Nono would say, "I don't know that this one's going to be any good—if I even live to see it." He turned 85 two weeks before the final in Qatar, so this World Cup reasonably could've been his last. Instinct told me that he'd want his eldest grandson beside him for the semifinal, despite the risk of breaking *cábala*. Haley, who refused to do as the other women in my family and clutch rosary beads or light candles to the saints and sit in darkness away from the TV, turned the game on in my parents' apartment upstairs. The kids napped, ignorant of their father's anguish. And after 90 heart-pounding minutes, Nono and I exhaled. Argentina won 3–0.

The night before the final, I fell asleep to a YouTube video of Messi playing soccer as a 12-year-old in Rosario. Hours later, I woke up sweating and nervous, with a strange feeling in my stomach. Haley and the children had smiles on their faces, the day ahead as bright as any other. I started to feel that my insistence on the *cábala* that would separate us for the next two hours was ridiculous. *Maybe I could go and watch the final with Haley and her family,* I thought. That way, if we won, we could all celebrate together.

That's what a proper husband and father would do. They wouldn't abandon their family to walk into the lion's den alone. I was still thinking I should go with them as I wrapped an Argentinean flag around my shoulders and watched Haley dress the kids in their matching blue-and-white jerseys and tracksuits. But my wife, as she usually does, knew better. She encouraged me to stay strong. I watched them leave through the basement door a few minutes before 10 a.m. The moment to suffer had come.

Argentina scored in the 23rd minute from the penalty spot. And by the time the ball reset after Ángel Di María scored their second goal in the 36th minute, the burden had started to lighten from my shoulders. A new, totally foreign sensation began to take shape in my body. I think it was . . . happiness. From the opening whistle of every game after the loss to Saudi Arabia, I felt that I was being crushed under the weight of a container ship. Even when Argentina scored a goal, I'd celebrate and then go right back to biting my fingernails and tapping nervously as the dog eyeballed me in bewilderment. During halftime against France, with Argentina up 2–nil, Haley texted to ask how I was doing. I replied, "If this result holds, I'll go there for the ceremony at the end. I want to be with you and the children."

I was still barefoot and in sweatpants at that point. So as the TV commentators heaped praise on Argentina and declared that once the trophy was in his hands Lionel Messi would be the undisputed greatest player in history, I grabbed the keys to the Honda Civic, pulled out a pair of jeans, socks, and sneakers, and placed them in a pile beside me on the couch. That way, I was ready to run out the garage door 45 minutes and six seconds later, once the final whistle blew.

Cábalas are nonsense when you're winning. They open your eyes to how childish and insignificant you are—a grown man practicing witchcraft in the suburbs of East Tennessee. A day before the final, the Argentine-American journalist Lucía Benavides—also following *cábala*, like tens of millions of Argentines worldwide—tweeted the link to a *New York Times* story about the army of witches casting spells to protect Messi and the national team from their many enemies. *Brian, you're too smart to believe this*, I told myself while reading it. *You have a master's degree and a subscription to* The New Yorker. *Nothing bad is going to happen because you put your socks on.*

For years, my mom cast spells to rid me of indigestion and the evil eye. I manipulated her superstition to get picked up early from school when the nurse could detect nothing physically wrong with me and I wanted to get out of tests I hadn't studied for. *Superstition is for the poor and uneducated*, I declared. And yet, in the 81st minute, moments after Mbappé scored a supernatural goal to level the score at 2–2, I tossed my car keys across the room, flung my clothes off the couch, and dropped to my knees, pleading with God to forgive me for ignorantly believing that I couldn't affect the outcome of the World Cup final.

And He heard me.

With the weight of 100 million Argentinians and Bangladeshis on his shoulders and an entire universe propelling him to the one trophy that had evaded him over his 19-year professional career, Messi was finally a World Cup champion. The tears that had dried as Mbappé stepped up to take his penalty erupted like lava, burning my eyelids and turning my cheeks red. After Haley FaceTimed me with Alba and Enzo, the first call I made was to Nono. He didn't answer, so I called my mom, begging her to give him the phone. When she got to him, Nono was in the backyard—he had walked away from the game at 2–2, fearing he would have a heart attack. I told him over tears, "*Nono, lo hicimos. Argentina ganó el Mundial. Somos campeones del mundo. No lo puedo creer. SOMOS CAMPEONES DEL MUNDO.*" And he and I cried together, 700 miles apart but closer than we'd ever been before.

I've repeated those same words—*We are world champions*—10,000 times since December 18, 2022.

The 2022 World Cup final in Qatar is hailed as the best, or the most dramatic, in history. It was a clash of titans: Messi vs. Mbappé, two of the greatest soccer players alive today, swinging back and forth like prizefighters. This was precisely what Qatar paid an eye-popping $220 billion for—at least $200 billion more than the next most expensive World Cup, Brazil's in 2014. Beyond anything that happened on the field, the final was a spectacle, with elaborate processions and ceremonies, songs and costumes, politicians and celebrities that the cameras scanned for unendingly, just as they do during the Super Bowl and Wimbledon and every important final of every important sport in the world.

In the midst of my elation, I couldn't help thinking about those things: *Who was this event really for? Who does this game really belong to?* I thought of the thousands of Argentinians who sold their cars and emptied their life savings to travel to Qatar and somehow, through witchcraft or bribery, got tickets to the game. Nosebleed seats at the Super Bowl start at $6,800. Seats behind the goal for the final in Qatar were $33,000. You and I are not supposed to be inside these modern coliseums. They're a billionaire's playground. It's baffling that they even let in the 22 players who over 120 minutes emptied themselves and sacrificed their bodies—as if the spectacle were forced to make way for the inconvenience of the game itself.

And yet, despite everything that I know about the Qatari World Cup—the bloodshed, the graves dug by orphaned sons who gave their fathers so wealthier men could make their statement to the world—I am still overcome with emotion. Every time I recall Gonzalo Montiel scoring the winning penalty kick and Messi finally kissing the golden trophy, I dissolve into a sea of tears. When Enzo woke us up crying for milk at 2:30 that night, Haley told me I turned to her, my eyes still shut, and whispered softly in her ear, "*Campeones del mundo.*"

I cannot unlink the joy I feel today from the sorrow of not being in Argentina, with my aunts and uncles, cousins and friends, to make memories of the celebration. I watched the videos of Buenos Aires and Rosario they sent me over WhatsApp; the Instagram algorithm, picking up on my obsession, feeds me new videos, even months later, every time I log on. I view them enviously. Because I know this joy will not last forever. The morning after the final, Juan, a friend from Entre Rios, reminded me in a WhatsApp message that the men's World Cup has been played 22 times, nearly every four years since 1930. Argentina has made six finals, including the first and the most recent, and won three times. It's very possible that, like Nono, I will not see the country of my ancestors triumphant ever again. This may have been the last wild celebration from the podium of illusion—the last footballing dream turned to reality before I die. I've prayed that God would send me bursting forward in time so I could immediately begin to feel nostalgia for that moment. I long to tell my grandchildren the story of the 2022 World Cup final, just as Nono told me of the finals of 1950,1962, 1978, and 1986.

I imagine they will gather around my feet before the 2058 tournament, held on a lunar colony or in North Korea, and beg me to tell them about Messi, Di María, and the other gray-haired men with bushy mustaches they've seen reminiscing about that December in Qatar when they were immortal. And this is what I'll say:

I watched alone from the basement. After 90 minutes, I was on death's doorstep, moments from leaving your grandmother a widow and your parents orphans. But by a miracle, God saved me. I drove to be with them, as fast as I could. I hugged

them tight and cried with them in my arms. Because the
were no other Argentinians around, instead of recounting t
final over *mate* or drinking bottles of Malbec late into t
night, we went to eat at a Mexican restaurant on Clint
Highway where the owner gifted us raspberry tequila sho
to toast the victory. But I didn't care. Because my sufferi
had finally been rewarded. My nightmare was over. I sa
Argentina champion of the world. And I will never forget

'Ni de Aquí, Ni de Allá'

El árbol que tú olvidaste siempre se acuerda de ti
Y le pregunta a la noche si serás o no feliz
El arroyo me ha contado que el árbol suele decir
Quien se aleja junta queja en vez de quedarse aquí.

—Atahualpa Yupanqui

A story about Lionel Messi went viral in Argentina the week after the 2022 World Cup final. Its author, Hernán Casciari, read a condensed version, which he titled "Lionel's Suitcase," on a national radio program in the days between the final and Christmas. The story is about Messi's journey from being a 13-year-old boy who left Argentina for Spain after his family could no longer afford the medical treatment he needed to grow normally to the man who captained his nation to its first World Cup trophy in 36 years.

A video of Casciari reading the story appeared on YouTube. Soon after, Messi—who was back home in Rosario for the holidays—sent a voice message to the radio station telling them that his wife, Antonella, had shown him a clip on Instagram, and they cried together while listening to it. Like Messi, I cried when I heard Casciari read the story for the first time. In fact, Casciari—who had immigrated like the Messis and thousands of other Argentinians to Barcelona just before the country's economic collapse in 2001—cried while narrating it.

During his time in Europe, Messi became an ambassador for Argentinians abroad. Even though Spain had attempted to persuade him to switch allegiance and play for their national team when he was still a teenager, he resisted acclimating to his new country. He sought to be Argentinian, despite the criticisms of his compatriots for not being Argentinian enough, especially after their loss to Germany in the 2014 World Cup final. In the media outlets of Buenos Aires, they called for him never to return home. But that was impossible. Because Messi, like so many immigrants, had kept his suitcase packed and his eye on the front door from the moment he landed in Spain.

Immigration has been at the forefront of my life, even before I moved away from home in 2011. Bayonne, the city in New Jersey where I grew up, is a place of resettled departures. You're as likely to hear Spanish, Polish, or Arabic on the street as English. My own home was divided: upstairs, where I lived with my parents and brother, we mainly spoke our second tongue; downstairs, my maternal grandparents spoke only Spanish. So I had no choice but to be fluent if I wanted to have a relationship with them.

I've always been curious why people, including my family, come to America just to create time capsules of the places they left behind. If 1970s Argentina had been cryogenically frozen and thawed into a house on 19th Street in Bayonne decades later, that was my home. We drank *mate cocido*, a tea brewed with yerba mate leaves from South America, and cooked extravagant *asados*, or barbecues, on the traditional Argentine grill my dad had built in the backyard. We spoke with the hard *shh* sound people from the River Plate basin make when pronouncing the double l (as in *ella* or *silla*), and listened to zambas from folk singers like Atahualpa Yupanqui and Jorge Cafrune. When I was five, my father dressed me in a Boca Juniors kit he'd bought on a trip back home and took pictures for the family. Later I chose to support Rosario Central, a less famous club from my grandfather's city that I fell in love with because of his stories of watching them in good times and bad throughout the 1950s and '60s. A sticker with their blue-and-yellow crest is on the water bottle I drink from as I write this.

Even though I had access through my family to a world that was five thousand miles away, I wished we had gone to Argentina more often. Every summer, the Spanish kids flew to Galicia while I languished in Bayonne. It was a time before Skype, YouTube, or WhatsApp. My only connections to Argentina were skirt steaks and chorizos, Gabriel Batistuta, and the sportscaster Andrés Cantor (he of the half-minute *¡Gooooooooooool!* calls).

By January, weeks after the 2022 World Cup final, I'd listened to "Lionel's Suitcase" a dozen times. I was listening again with my headphones on while I unpacked boxes in the basement of the house we had bought in north Knoxville, where I watched Gonzalo Montiel score the winning penalty to give Argentina its victory against France. In one of the boxes, I found a copy of a story I had written for a Spanish literature class my junior year at William Paterson University. In college, I majored in Latin American and Latino studies because I longed to connect with my parents, my grandparents, and the people they left behind in a land I felt a part of despite having spent so little time in. For that lit class, Professor Rodriguez assigned us to write one original short story entirely in Spanish. I wrote mine about Nono, my maternal grandfather, who baptized me *Cabezón*, harassed me at soccer games until high school, and taught me how to tell a story.

Nono fascinated and confounded me. For years before I left, he captivated me with stories of soccer and his childhood in Rosario, the same city where Messi was born. He'd narrate them for me like he was giving a lecture broadcast to millions over the radio, even though it was just us at the kitchen table, drinking wine and eating Lay's chips and cold cuts. But as much as he let me know him through his lectures, he was still an enigma. He would fall asleep muttering to himself with repetitions of Yankees baseball games or cowboy Westerns on mute in the background. And when he'd speak about the

Argentina of his past, he'd do it with an affection he didn't feel for the U.S., a country he had become a citizen of despite speaking only enough English to greet the mail carrier. He was unsettled and disillusioned, and I thought I knew why: he needed to go back home while there was still time.

Nono dismissed the idea, saying it was too late to go back. The parents and grandparents of my Dominican and Mexican friends had built wealth in America so they could return to their towns and villages with luxuries that had escaped them as children. Nono had come to this country, accumulated few luxuries, and decided this would be the place where he'd die. Whenever I prodded him about returning to Rosario, he would quote a line from the Argentine folk singer Facundo Cabral: *No soy ni de aquí ni de allá*—I'm from everywhere. I'm from nowhere.

I titled the story I wrote for Professor Rodriguez's class *El Hombre Viejo* ("The Old Man"). It opens with the same lines that open this story. They were written by the folk legend Atahualpa Yupanqui, whom Nono would often listen to while lying on the couch in his living room with his eyes closed. The lines translate to "The tree you've forgotten always remembers you. And it asks the night whether or not you're happy. The river tells me that the tree often says, 'Whoever leaves collects grief instead of staying here.'"

I wrote most of "The Old Man" while lying on the same floral couch where Nono listened to that song. The story opens with him sitting there, reflecting on the lines as they ring out from the cassette player nearby, and follows him through an average day in his life: arguing with my grandmother, going outside to water the plants, and talking with me at the kitchen table as a soccer game plays on the TV in the background. Inner dialogue runs throughout the story, with Nono asking himself if he should have stayed in Rosario and questioning whether the exchange of countries was worth it as he nears his final days. Inside of him, a tug of war is taking place between his monotonous life in New Jersey and the one he still had time for in the home he'd never forgotten.

Most of the story takes place in a dream after Nono fell asleep listening to Yupanqui. I shout him awake, reminding him that he promised that very day we'd buy airplane tickets to Argentina so I could watch Rosario Central play. (We took this trip together in 2009, a year after I wrote the story.) I printed out "The Old Man," clipped the sheets together, and gave the manuscript to Nono as a Father's Day present. I'm not sure how the story wound up back in my possession. Maybe he returned it to me with instructions on where to make changes to the grammar and vocabulary or rewrite the action. Or maybe I printed out a second copy and hid it away so I could find it and remember those years when I still believed, naively, that going back in time was possible.

I wish I could peel back the layers of my own identity—being American, Northern, from New Jersey, and of Bayonne, and at the same time, Latino, South American, Argentinian, and Rosarian. The layers stack on top of one another, sometimes sliding into place like puzzle pieces and other times more like colors splattered on a blank canvas. Being told by my parents that I'm American because I was born here and by strangers in Tennessee that I'm not because of the places my family tree traces back to. It's a bizarre experience growing up in Hudson County, where everyone seemed to be from somewhere else, then moving to Knoxville, where peoples' roots stretch back to the Mayflower. I often joke that I moved to the TV version of America, with its blue-eyed blonde girls, sweeping suburbs, and country music, only once I'd left New Jersey, eager to write my own story, as my parents, grandparents, and great-grandparents had written theirs before me.

My connection to Bayonne, where I lived for 22 years, will likely sever when my parents leave or die. I may only go back to show my children, telling them as we drive through the sea of red lights, "Appreciate how good you have it, because you could have been born here, where the breeze smells of sewage, the sirens blare past midnight, and a parking spot close to your house is as hard to find as a stranger who smiles back inside Shop Rite." But that city is tattooed onto me, together with all the other markings that make me who I am.

When I went back to New Jersey that first November after I'd left for Knoxville, friends told me I spoke with the hint of a Southern accent. I recoiled. I fought (I fight) so hard to say *youse* instead of *y'all, pie* instead of *pizza,* to care when the New York Giants make a playoff run (and to remind people that they play in New Jersey). Like Messi in Casciari's story, I fight to preserve my accent, just as I've fought to refine a very specific kind of Spanish despite being raised around all other

kinds of Spanish speakers, so the Hondurans and Colombia
I play soccer with at the park will pause and ask, "Are y
Argentinian?" and Argentinians will ask, "Are you Rosaric

I envy the people who stay—who are from and of the sar
place. And yet I know how many people wish they h
other origins to return to. I remember the disappointment
Haley's face when she got her 23&Me results and they re
99.1 percent white. "Just like everyone else in East Tennesse
she said—a British girl with enough French mixed in to tu
her skin bronze in the summertime.

I want to ask every person I meet in a church pew or at t
playground with my children about where they came fro
where they've been, and what their struggle has looked li
On the one hand, I'm curious. But I also know personally hc
complicated identity can be. I wonder how other immigrar
and transplants maintain their customs. Do they drink *ye*
mate from a calabash gourd in the afternoon or settle for a c
of black coffee? Are their offices covered in flags and pictur
of places they escape to when they're feeling blue? Do th
lie back on the couch, like Nono, soaking in the sounds
home? Or are they like Lionel Messi, with his suitcase rig
beside the door, always ready to take the next flight back
Rosario?

Lionel's Suitcase

The following is my translation of the condensed version of Hernán Casciari's "Lionel's Suitcase," which is available in Spanish on YouTube, Spotify, and Apple Podcasts. A longer version of the story was published in Orsai *magazine in February 2023.*

Saturday mornings in 2003, TV3 in Catalonia would broadcast games from FC Barcelona's youth teams. And in the conversations between Argentinians who had left and resettled in Spain, there were two questions that were repeated endlessly: How do you make *dulce de leche* by boiling cans of condensed milk—that was the first question because we were desperate—and at what time did the 15-year-old from Rosario who scored goals in every game play? Those were the two most important questions.

During the 2003–04 season, Lionel Messi played 37 games across four youth and senior teams for Barcelona. He scored 35 goals. I remember the TV ratings for the Saturday mornings when he played were better than the prime-time numbers. There was already talk about this kid, the Future No. 10. In the barbershops, bars, and the stands of Camp Nou, people spoke about who he was and where he'd come from. The only one who didn't speak was him. In the postgame interviews, he'd respond to every question with a simple *sí* or *no*. Sometimes he'd thank the interviewer. And then he'd look down at his feet.

The displaced Argentines, the immigrants, would ha
preferred a loudmouth. That was more familiar to us than
quiet boy. But there was something gratifying for us whe
finally, Messi would piece together a sentence. Because he
swallow all the *s*'s. He'd say *fúl* instead of *falta* and *gambe*
instead of *regate*. And we felt relieved, for we had discover
that kid was one of us. He was one of the immigrants wl
had never put away their suitcase.

I should explain this. At that time in Barcelona, there we
two types of immigrants. There were the ones who, after th
airplane had touched down in Barajas or Prat, tucked th
suitcases away in a closet, far in the corner, forgetting abo
Argentina. And they started to say *vale*, *tío*, *hostia* immediate
Then there were those of us who had our suitcases ju
inside the door. We never put them away. We preserved o
customs—for example, drinking *mate*, our *yeísmo*. All t
time, we'd say *shuvia* (rain), *cashe* (street), so that we'd nev
forget to speak with the *yé*.

Time passed, for everyone. And suddenly Messi, the teenag
who didn't talk, became the undisputed No. 10 for Barcelor
With his ascension came league championships, Copas c
Rey, Champions League trophies. Yet he knew, as mu
as we did—the other immigrants—that the hardest thing
maintain, above all else, was his accent. It wasn't easy to ke
saying *gambeta* instead of *regate*. Because when time pass
you become embedded in the society that took you in. Y
merge with your surroundings. Yet we also understood th
this was our last stand: maintaining our way of speaking. Ar

incredibly, Messi was our leader in battle. The kid who didn't speak kept alive our way of speaking.

So suddenly we weren't just enjoying the greatest soccer player we had ever seen—because going to Camp Nou in those days was unbelievable. But we were on guard, making sure some Spanish slang hadn't found its way into his vernacular. That it didn't show up in an interview. We celebrated when he kept speaking the same way. And beyond his goals, we celebrated that in the dressing room, he always had his thermos and his *mate*.

Out of nowhere, Messi became Barcelona's most famous person. But just like us, he never stopped being an Argentinian in some other place. The Argentinian flag he carried to celebrate every European Cup fascinated us, as did his stance when he traveled to represent Argentina in Beijing in 2008 to win Olympic gold for Argentina without the club's permission. His Christmas holidays were spent in Rosario despite having to play a tournament in Camp Nou in early January. Everything he did was like a subliminal message to us, those who in 2000 had arrived with him in Barcelona. It is very hard to explain how much it meant for those of us who lived so far away from home: How he had carried us up from the apathy of the dreary world we lived in. How he, a kid who didn't speak, helped us to never forget our place in the world. To hold tight to our compasses. Messi made us happy in a way that was so peaceful and pure that when the insults began to arrive from Argentina we couldn't make sense of them.

Spineless. They said *You only care about money.* They told him *Stay in Europe, mercenary. You don't feel the shirt. You're Spanish, not Argentinian. If you quit once, think about quitting again. You're not one of us.*

For 15 years, I lived far away from my country, and I swear that I never endured a nightmare like hearing voices of disdain from the place I love most in the world. There is no pain more unbearable than hearing from your son or daughter the words Messi heard from his son Thiago when he was six years old: *Daddy, why do they hate you in Argentina?*

My voice is breaking. I can't catch my breath. I have two daughters—one is Argentinian, the other Catalan—and if either one of them were to say something like that to me, I'd burn with resentment. I don't know how I'd go on living. That's why Messi's decision in 2016 to retire from the national team was almost a relief for us, the immigrants. We couldn't bear to watch him suffer any more because we knew how much he loved Argentina. We knew, from the time he was 15, the incredible effort he made to continue being Argentinian. To not sever the umbilical cord. When he retired in 2016, it was as if suddenly Messi had decided to remove his hands from the fire. But not just his—ours also. Because the criticisms from those assholes back home burned us too.

And it's at that moment of the story that the most unusual and extraordinary thing in modern football happened. The evening of June 26, 2016, when Messi decided he was done with the insults and abandoned the national team, a

15-year-old boy wrote him a letter on Facebook. And it ended with this line: *Consider staying, Lionel. But stay so that you can enjoy yourself—which is what these people want to take from you.*

Seven years later, the boy who wrote that card—Enzo Fernández—was the standout young player of the World Cup won by Lionel Messi. Because Messi returned almost immediately to the national team. And he announced that he did it so that all the children who wrote him letters and shared messages on social media knew that giving up is not an option in life. Upon returning, he won everything there was left to win for his country. Everything that he dreamed of winning. And he silenced the voices of his critics.

Not all of them, of course. Because some, including during this very World Cup, found him, for the first time ever, to be vulgar. It was after the Holland match when he said, *Que mirá, bobo. Andá payá, bobo.* (Essentially, Messi was saying, "What are you looking at, dimwit? Go stand in the corner.") For those of us, the immigrants who had monitored his accent for more than 15 years, that sentence was perfect. Because he swallowed all his *s*'s. Because his accent was intact. It soothed us to confirm that he was still the same kid who helped preserve our joy when we were an ocean away from home.

Now some of us have returned. Some remain in Spain. But all of us have savored watching Messi return to Argentina with the World Cup trophy in the suitcase he had never stowed away. Because that suitcase has remained by his door from the day he stepped foot in Europe.

This epic story would have never occurred if the 15-year-old Messi had tucked his luggage in his closet and succumbed to the pressure of saying *vale, tío, hostia*. But he never confused his accent. He never forgot his place in the world. For that reason, all of humanity desired with such passion to see Messi finally win this. Because never, in the long list of humanity's greatest heroes, had we seen a man like him standing atop the summit of the world. A simple boy. One like any of us. This December, as in every year before, Messi left Qatar, as he had left Spain and France, to spend Christmas with his family in Rosario. Like always. To wave to his neighbors. To play with his children. His habits are unchanged. His customs remain the same. The only thing that is different is what he brought in his suitcase.

An Email from 2043

*People like us, who believe in physics, know that the
distinction between past, present and future is only a
stubbornly persistent illusion.*

—Albert Einstein

One morning last July, I was sitting at my desk drinking
coffee and trying to write. It was 6 a.m., and every
room in the house was dark as Haley and the children slept
oblivious to the sound of my typing coming from the lamp-lit
office. Motivation had come slowly, and I was groggy from
sleep. So after a few minutes of trying and failing to come up
with an idea for a story, I turned to procrastination, opening
my Chrome browser and switching back and forth between
Facebook, Twitter, and Wikipedia. After deleting about a
hundred emails from my Gmail promotions folder, I clicked
over to the primary tab just as a new email with a little yellow
banner beside the sender's name popped up at the top.

It was the email address that made me pause. It was from alba.elena15@gmail.com. *No way,* I thought. Alba Elena is my three-year-old daughter who was, at that moment, asleep one room over from my office.

"This is for real, Dad," the subject read. Suddenly the haze of sleep fully lifted. "This is for real" is the kind of thing a Nigerian prince or Russian spambot writes to get you to download a computer virus you then have to pay them in cryptocurrency to remove. I listen to *This American Life*; I wasn't born yesterday.

The email was dated February 3, 2043—a day before my 54th birthday. I pushed back against my doubt, took a deep breath, and clicked. This is what Alba wrote me.

Hi Daddy,

You may not believe that it's really me writing you this. And I won't be able to convince you that I'm telling the truth. Just try to think of it like that movie you like with Amy Adams and the aliens. You don't have to understand how they communicate with each other to understand what's happening. You always say you can tell if a movie or a book or a goal is good if it makes you feel something.

The reason I'm emailing you is that yesterday I was scrolling back through the pages of dispatches you started writing in

2021—that was only last year for you, just before Enzo was born. You've always written us letters and love poems. You never want to watch us read them, but you ask Mom after to find out if we smiled or cried. Mom keeps the ones from when we were little in a box underneath your bed.

For years, you wrote those dispatches. Around the time I was 13, you went quiet for a while. But two years ago, you started again, writing late into the night. Mom would tell you that if you were gonna stay up past midnight writing to just sleep on the mattress in the office downstairs because you were gonna wake her up when you walked into the bedroom. "Someone could sneeze in Siberia, and it'd wake your mom up," you'd whisper to me, winking, before heading back down with a cup of decaf coffee.

Mom is in the garage right now doing CrossFit with her friends; I can hear the barbell smacking against the ground every five seconds. She's good. Enzo's good, too. He left for Zagreb on Tuesday to sign a contract. That's not why I'm writing. I've got a message for you, Dad. But I have to be careful about what I say. There are rules about what you can and cannot know.

The future's nothing like what you pictured in your stories. In 2037, President McConaughey signs this new law that does away with money. Now money is time. It gets direct deposited into your bank at the start of every month; you keep it stored on a debit card and track it online. It's going to cost me three-and-a-half years to send you this email. That's 12

months standard, plus six additional months for every five ye
back in time the recipient is, plus a month for every 50 wo
I go over the limit.

Fortunately, I've got this covered. I'm gonna be 23 in th
weeks, Dad! And I know you're grinding your teeth
this point in the letter because I'm burying the lead. You
thinking did all the dreams you had for me come true?

I'll start with the good news: I'm not married to a guy w
political stickers on his pickup truck. My boyfriend does
have a tattoo on his face. But he does read your stor
before coming over to meet you, and he tries quoting C.
Lewis—though he gets it wrong, and it's a little awkwa
until you break the ice and ask him to pick a book from yo
library. I spend much of my free time painting, mostly bi
and mountains, with your Spotify playlists on as backgrou
noise. The house is covered in canvases. I went to Patagonia l
year with the girls from my soccer team and took a picture f
you at that place you love from *The Motorcycle Diaries*, whe
Che Guevara and his friend say they'd open a clinic at the ed
of the lake. And we all went to Scotland when I turned sev
and took a picture in front of the *Fàilte gu Alba* sign.

There is other news that isn't so good. One day, somethi
happens—the company I'm paying to send this won't let
tell you what—and it seems like half the world gets sick. No
of us get it at first. And then one day, your head starts to hu
and your left hand won't stop shaking. You get old quick
I bring you books at the hospital, and you annoy the nur

with jingles. You watch me on TV. Enzo filmed you watching me play once when he was back home visiting and sent it to me. You were screaming and crying like in the video Mom showed us after Argentina won the World Cup in 2022 when you held us in your arms.

So you know, Dad, nothing changes because I sent you this email. I'm not allowed to tell you anything that you have the power to change. But I can tell you that when we get a little older than we are right now in your timeline, birthdays with you get really fun. You let us pick out a movie to see at the theatre together. We go to museums; by the time I'm 17, there are trains that let us travel at hyperspeed from Knoxville to the Met and the Smithsonians. If the weather's nice, really early we take the boat to a pretty spot on the river, and Mom tangles up all the fishing line, and you laugh as you untangle it. You keep pictures of the fish we catch—even the little ones—and hang them in the library.

A couple of years from when you're reading this, your hair starts to go and your muscles ache, so you rub Vicks all over and make the house smell like eucalyptus cigarettes (Mom hates that, by the way). But you're happy. You say we're your little tribe, even when we're teenagers and don't want to take pictures with you at the Grand Canyon, or we hang out with kids whose parents let them drink in the basement. You never excommunicate us. Mom says she gets all the credit for making you so patient; you say you had no choice, then wink, and I see all your wrinkles.

So that you know this isn't a joke, I paid a company to retrieve a picture for me. In the future, since so many people from your generation stopped making photo albums and hanging pictures, I can pay a company—another one, not the one I'm paying to send this email—and they'll go back through your social media to find pictures and videos. It's like uncovering relics from the past because, despite the sickness and the natural disasters and the polar bears going extinct, the future does get better in one way: Instagram doesn't exist anymore.

Do you remember how as a kid, I'd steal your phone and roam around the house, taking pictures of the walls and videotaping Enzo eating the dirt out of the flowerpots? I'm attaching the one you captioned "Self-Portrait of the Artist at 2," back when my cheeks were chubby and my hair was blonde. I don't know why you didn't print that photo out, Dad! I got the rule of thirds right, and I couldn't even spell my name yet.

I'm way past my word count now. So I just wanted to say, don't change, Dad. It's all going to turn out just like it's supposed to. You raised us Presbyterian for a reason, right? "The story's already written," you always said. "You can't change what's coming. You've just got to keep your gaze pointed up and your feet moving forward." I promise there are no storms coming that we won't make it through.

Oh, and Mom says to keep taking your multivitamins.

With all the love in the world,

Your Albita

P.S. Don't try to write back; it won't go through—something about a firewall, like in China.

I finished reading and, even though she said not to, the first thing I did was hit "Reply." I wrote quickly: "Alba, is this really you? But you're sleeping in the crib in the other room. You're a baby! If this is some kind of joke, I'm not mad at all. Please tell me the truth. Who wrote this?"

The email kicked back 30 seconds later, "Recipient server did not accept your request," just as she had said it would.

I sat at my desk with my head in my hands. Then I got up and walked over to her bedroom. The blinds were still down and light was just creeping into the house. The white noise machine was on full blast when I put my ear to her door. It was just past seven. I didn't hear rustling but walked in anyway and stood by the crib. I pulled apart the curtains just enough for a stream of morning light to enter; I could see Alba lying belly down in a jumble of stuffed animals. She opened her eyes. "*Buendía* baby," I said. "Did you have a good *noni?*"

Rubbing her face, she responded, "Where's Mommy?"

I asked this toddler version of my daughter—the only version of her I'd known before that morning—if I could pick her up. She nodded. So I grabbed her and held her in the chair beside the crib. She tucked her head into my chest, both of us with our eyes closed, mine spilling tears.

"Self-Portrait of the Artist at 2"
by Alba Elena Canever

Acknowledgements

I finished this book just after my third child, Elio, came home from the NICU at UT Medical Center. I dreamed it up in 2022 after being inspired by the books Argentine writer Hernán Casciari had published comprising older stories he'd rewritten or adapted for new audiences. After publishing dozens of stories to Substack and other blogs over the past three years, I decided to take some of my favorites, work with a close friend and professional editor, and publish them independently, just like my high school band did demo tapes we were bold enough to mail to record labels.

In a way, a printed book legitimizes a writer. More importantly, it checks an item off my bucket list and provides my children with something real they can one day touch, as I have photos and keepsakes from my parents and grandparents.

These acknowledgments will be brief. The biggest thank you goes to my wife, Haley, who endures my delusions and yet chooses to be kind, gracious, and encouraging, as well as many other positive things. I do not make life easy for her, but we both knew we weren't signing up to be bored when we exchanged vows.

I must also thank my parents, Adriana and Oscar, for all their support. Having a 34-year-old son self-publish a book of stories does not fall high on any immigrant parent's bucket list. But they've always taken an interest and encouraged me to pursue my love of writing and books, even if it meant earning college degrees that were essentially useless in the real world.

This book is dedicated to Nono, my real-life grandfather. I've not fibbed in any of my descriptions of him. One day, I will write another book, *Things My Grandfather Told Me*. It might do better as a comedy routine (though it will probably be rated NC-17). My grandmother, Nona, should also be acknowledged, as she's suffered the same fate as Haley, being married to a deluded storyteller who hogs the television for days at a time to watch soccer games.

The only reason these stories read coherently is due to the masterful editing of Donna Spencer, who has donated too much valuable time to the herculean effort of constraining and clarifying my nonsense. Buy this book so I can repay her tremendous sacrifice. I cannot imagine my writing without Donna's careful guidance and surgeon-like precision.

I could turn this into a list of people I love and like. But I'm lucky if you made it this far. So I'll keep the rest short.

I'm grateful to my best friends, Mickey and Jeremy. I was always the weakest link in the chain. Without their ambition and successes, I wouldn't have been motivated to pursue my own. I look forward to a future where we're old and gray, seated at a table reminiscing just as we did as teenagers.

In my 20s, I added another best friend, my brother Victor. One day we realized we loved the same books, films, and combat sports, despite having virtually no crossover of friend groups or hobbies in our adolescence. Knowing that he's one of my faithful readers keeps me humble and honest.

If you've ever shared my work, wrote me about a story, or came to a reading at Bear Den Books—thank you. More than 150 people are subscribed to *Storytime with Big Head*. Seeing your names encourages me to keep going when I feel like no one is listening. I should also thank anyone who appears in my stories. I didn't ask your permission. But I hope you've gotten a laugh out of this.

Last of all, the person who played the most important role in my journey to Substack and eventually publishing *Big Head on the Block* is Chris Echols, who gave me a copy of Austin Kleon's *Show Your Work* in 2021 and told me to not ask for permission to chase after my dreams. This book would not exist without the invaluable conversations we had about what my writing life could like while eating greasy tacos at Esperanza.